By Any
Illegal Means

By Donald MacKenzie

Donald MacKenzie

By Any
Illegal Means

A CRIME CLUB BOOK
DOUBLEDAY
New York   London   Toronto   Sydney   Auckland

A Crime Club Book
PUBLISHED BY DOUBLEDAY
a division of Bantam Doubleday Dell Publishing Group, Inc.
666 Fifth Avenue, New York, New York 10103

DOUBLEDAY and the portrayal of a man
with a gun are trademarks of Doubleday,
a division of Bantam Doubleday Dell
Publishing Group, Inc.

Library of Congress Cataloging-in-Publication Data

MacKenzie, Donald, 1918–
   By any illegal means / Donald MacKenzie.
     p. cm.
   "A Crime Club book."
   I. Title.
PR9199.3.M325B9   1990
813'.54—dc20   89-29691
CIP

ISBN 0-385-41236-3

July 1990
First Edition in the United States of America

A book for Erika

*By Any
Illegal Means*

ONE

ASSASSINATION ATTEMPT AGAINST PINOCHET

SA PRESS SANTIAGO   President Pinochet on Sept. 7 escaped with only slight hand injuries from an assassination attempt. Several hours later, General Molina, chief of the Centro Nacional de Informaciones, announced the immediate introduction of a state of siege. Opponents of the régime were arrested and restrictions imposed on the news media.

The assassination attempt, which left five of the presidential guard dead and eleven injured, occurred as the President's motorcade was ambushed while crossing a bridge southeast of Santiago on the return journey from his weekend residence in Melicotón 44 km from the capital. Four terrorists, armed with automatic weapons, blocked the motorcade's passage but concentrated their fire on a decoy car in front of the vehicle in which Pinochet was traveling. The President's car was hit by thirty-two bullets, all of which failed to pierce the bulletproof windows. Some damage was done by a hand-grenade. All four terrorists were killed at the scene of the attempted assassination. In a television appearance in the

early hours of Sept. 8, the President appealed for calm
and declared war against Marxism and other international organisations that spread "sinister and distorted
information against Chile."

Roland van Hall turned away from the doors that opened onto
the balcony. His room was on the tenth floor of the Chaco Hotel.
A hundred feet below, jacarandas, rubber and orange trees
shielded the stone benches in the Plaza Uruguaya from the fierce
afternoon heat. Blossom scented the exhausted air. The city was
built on a low hill overlooking the east bank of the Rio Paraguay.
It was laid out in Spanish Colonial fashion. Half-empty skyscrap-
ers formed an uneven backdrop against the parched blue sky.

The airconditioning unit was set at fifty degrees Fahrenheit but
sweat rolled down van Hall's ribcage. He was forty-two years old
with thinning brown hair and a crafty intelligent face. He was
wearing a white drip-dry suit and two-tone shoes. His left arm
still ached from the jabs he had endured in London—tetanus and
typhoid were endemic in Paraguay. He opened his Gucci despatch case. A sheaf of thousand-dollar bills was lodged in a pocket
inside. He peeled off ten bills in readiness. These interviews always gave him a sense of uneasiness. This was the fourth, the
meetings always taking place outside Chile. The man he was
about to meet was Doctor Aníbal Mesquita, an official working in
the Foreign Department of the Banco de Chile.

Van Hall took the lift down to the lobby, where stone dolphins
spouted water into lily-topped pools, and tiled walls depicted
hunting scenes in the Gran Chaco jungle. A couple of Guarani
bellboys lounged near the lifts. Outside on the pavement, the
doorman was chatting to a lottery ticket vendor. Van Hall
glanced at his watch. It was siesta time. There was only one person in the lobby, a woman wearing dark glasses and sipping iced
coffee. Traffic would be light at this hour along the Alfredo
Stroesner Freeway to the airport; the journey would take no
longer than half-an-hour.

A cab drew up in front of the hotel entrance. The doorman cut
short his conversation and removed his peaked cap. A short fat
man emerged from the taxi and paid the driver, ignoring the
doorman's fulsome welcome. The new arrival carried no baggage.
He waddled into the lobby, turning his shortnecked head in all

directions. Van Hall lifted a hand and both men entered the lift. Neither spoke until they were safely behind van Hall's door. Van Hall's Spanish was grammatically correct although accented.

"Doctor Mesquita! A pleasure to see you!"

Their meetings always began in a parade of mutual compliments. The fat man sat down very carefully, placing plump hands on his knees. He counted the ten thousand dollars that van Hall gave him, holding each bill to the light and snapping the paper.

"It is just," he announced. He opened his nylon shirt and put the money in a canvas belt next to his skin. His brown face was lugubrious.

"Life has been difficult in the capital, Señor. It is true that the state of siege has been lifted but no man trusts another."

His manner was sly and avuncular, like a conjuror at a children's party. He groped in the recesses of his soiled jacket and swung an envelope between thumb and forefinger.

"Only four people have seen what you are about to see, Señor. One of them is my wife."

Van Hall extracted the typewritten sheet of paper from the envelope and read:

CENTRO NACIONAL DE INFORMACIONES

POST-MORTEM EXAMINATION

NAME: Unknown   APPARENT AGE: 30-35 years
IDENTIFIED BY: José Hidalgo, CAPTAIN, C.N.D.I.
DATE: Sept. 7
EXTERNAL EXAMINATION: The body was that of a well-nourished male. There were severe sectionings of the front of the body and intensive burning of the legs and hands downs to the muscles and tissue. There was fracture of both anklebones. There were no further means of identification
TIME OF DEATH: Found dead at 10.50 hrs Sept. 7
INTERNAL EXAMINATION:
   SKULL: There was extensive fracturing of the skull.
   MERINGERATE: The brain showed perforation on section. There was no evidence of natural dis-

ease that could have caused or contributed to death.

MOUTH: TONGUE: OESOPHAGUS: The air passages contained carbon deposit.

LARYNX: TRACHEA: LUNGS & PLEURAE: The lungs were congested with adhesions to the chest wall.

PERICARDIUM: HEART: The coronary vessels showed severe damage.

STOMACH: The stomach contained a partly digested meal.

PERITONEUM: INTESTINES: Normal.

GLANDS: LIVER & GALL-BLADDER: Revealed no abnormality.

GENERATIVE ORGANS: Healthy.

DID DEATH ARISE FROM NATURAL CAUSES? No.

DISEASE OR CONDITION DIRECTLY LEADING TO DEATH: Gunshot wounds to the head. Injuries to the skull conducive with use of a rifled weapon. The entrance wounds were inverted, the margins depressed. The exit wounds were everted. Pieces of bone were carried out by projectiles.

SIGNED: Ramón Palau Álvarez (Colonel-Doctor).

"How did you come by this?" asked van Hall.

The fat man half-closed his eyes. "Molina prepared the report on the attempted coup. He sat next to Pinochet at the mass of Thanksgiving. Pinochet thanked God for the loyalty of the C.N.D.I. My wife translated the report into English."

Van Hall was watching the pulse-beat in the Doctor's fleshy throat.

"Your money was well spent," said Mesquita. "The official line taken by the media blamed the F.N.P.R. A pack of lies! The four men who died in the attempt on Pinochet's life were foreigners. Their bodies were burned beyond recognition. There is more." He reached into his pocket again. His hand was trembling slightly as he offered two additional pieces of paper. "I shall leave it to you what this is worth."

Two addresses were typed on the top sheet. *Cyclops Security 670 Brompton Road London SW* and *Vanteris SA 29 bis Place Vendôme Paris.*

Mesquita nodded encouragement. "Banco de Chile estimates General Molina's personal fortune to be in excess of forty million dollars. Nine-tenths of this is held outside Chile. The rest is in Switzerland. Every cent of his money has passed through the firm of Vanteris SA. Vanteris SA is owned by Luis Ortega. Ortega is Molina's godson."

The noise from the pool on the roof was suddenly loud. Van Hall did his best to control his excitement.

"This requires careful thought," he said. He put the typescript in his despatch case. Mesquita had flown in by way of Montevideo. His return flight left in ninety minutes.

The Chilean placed both fists on his knees and heaved himself up.

"Is it permitted to make an observation before I leave?"

"Why not?" Van Hall waved a hand.

"I have a feeling that you are disappointed in me," said Mesquita.

Van Hall shook his head. "As long as I continue to give you money, you will know that I am not disappointed."

The Chilean smiled slyly, his eyes disappearing in the folds of his face.

"A payment of more than two million French francs was made by Vanteris SA to Cyclops Security in August last year. That was in August, five weeks before the attempt on the President's life. I tell you these things because you are a man of honor."

Van Hall perched on the end of the bed. "I take it that we're talking about still more money?"

"A bonus," said Mesquita. "Molina's godson will be meeting someone from Cyclops in Paris the day after tomorrow. The name of this person is Paul Sheffield. A conference room has been booked in the Continental Hotel. I do not know where these people will be staying."

A rush of adrenalin found van Hall's brain. "I will investigate these matters," he said. "If your information is accurate, we will come to some arrangement."

He turned the door-handle and glanced up and down the corridor. "Adiós," he said and closed the door. He turned the key in the lock. Molina was perfectly placed for the attempt on Pi-

nochet's life. It would have been natural for them to have gone to
the British for help. They had a long history of providing mercenaries. Pinochet's death would cause no tears to be shed. The
facts were simple. The coup had failed, and although Molina retained the President's confidence, one false move would destroy
him. Faced with proof of his involvement in the assassination
attempt, he would be forced to buy silence.

Van Hall picked up the phone and asked the operator for a
London number. A man's voice answered on the third ring.

"Discreet Enquiries, Henry Hobart speaking."

"Listen to me carefully," said van Hall. "I want you on the first
plane out of London for Paris. Book yourself into the Continental. I'll be at the Saint James and Albany. Meet me there at twelve
o'clock noon, your time. Better still, call me from the airport.
Ok?"

"Ok," Hobart said.

The plane landed one hour late at Orly. It was twelve degrees
colder than it had been in Paraguay and van Hall had no coat
with him, so he bought a Burberry on his way from the airport.
He checked into his usual room at the Saint James and Albany,
on the fourth floor overlooking the rue de Rivoli. He took a cab to
Executive Security on rue Lincoln and left with a leather case
containing two thousand dollars' worth of gadgetry. He was in
the bath when Hobart called from Charles de Gaulle.

"Room four-two-six," said van Hall. He shaved, dressed and
ordered coffee sent up.

Hobart arrived half-an-hour later.

"Sit down," said van Hall. "You take sugar and cream with
your coffee?"

"Both," Hobart said. He dropped into one of the two armchairs
and stretched out his legs. He was thirty years old with neat fair
hair and the narrow head of a collie. His closely set eyes were the
color of wet slate. He was wearing a raincoat of the type favored
by Italian students—long, black and voluminous. Underneath he
wore a blazer and grey flannel trousers.

Van Hall filled a cup with coffee and gave it to his visitor.

"How are you, Henry?"

"I've been a whole lot better," said Hobart. "I don't get enough
sleep."

"That's what keeps you lean and hungry," said van Hall.

Hobart's eyes strayed to the bag of electronic equipment on the bed. "I still don't get enough sleep."

"How long have we known one another?" Van Hall's voice was casual.

Hobart gave it some thought. "It's got to be three, four years."

"Four years in February," said van Hall. He had used Hobart a couple of dozen times, routine enquiries to begin with. Surveillance assignments followed, each one a further test of Hobart's character and intelligence.

"There's one thing I learned early on in life," van Hall said genially. "Never take a man at face value. I had you checked out three years ago."

Hobart nodded. "I thought you might have done."

"A full history," van Hall went on, "from the time you left the Christian Brothers in East Grinstead. You were expelled for cheating."

Hobart showed not the least sign of shame. "I was lazy."

"You were caught," said van Hall, "and that wasn't smart, Henry. Any more than that business in South Africa, conning a woman out of twenty-eight thousand pounds. You could have gone to jail for that."

Hobart grinned. "She'd have had a lot of problems with her husband if she'd gone to the police."

"Then the Rand School of Ballroom Dancing." Van Hall shook his head. "An instructor, no less! I never thought of you as a dancing man, Henry."

"I was young," Hobart said. "Young and skint."

"What you were, was a rogue," said van Hall.

"There's plenty of people like me," Hobart said. "It's the fear what might happen that keeps people straight. Knock out the fear and you'd have a lot more lawbreakers."

"That's a very cynical remark," said van Hall. He pointed at the bag on the bed. "How much do you know about bugging?"

"You mean electronic eavesdropping," said Hobart. He seemed to like the expression. "I've done my share of it, why?"

"You get your room all right?"

"I got it," said Hobart. "I called from the airport. They're holding it until two o'clock."

Van Hall opened the bag on the bed. "Ever seen anything like this before, Henry?"

Hobart leaned forward. "Not that particular model, no. But I've seen others like it."

Van Hall held the microphone in the palm of his hand. It was the size of a matchbox with a two-inch retractible aerial.

"You can attach this to wood or metal," he said. "Stick it behind a curtain, under a table, wherever. There are six conference rooms in the Continental Hotel. They're kept locked at night, opened at eight in the morning for cleaning. How's your Spanish?"

"My *Spanish?*" Hobart repeated. "I don't speak a word of it, why?"

"No problem," said van Hall. "Take a look at this."

The cordless earplug receiver was no bigger than a deaf-aid button. He pointed down at the tape-recording unit. "You can only use one at a time, the earplug or tape-recorder. Once you're sure that you're getting your sound, you switch on to the tape." He demonstrated the controls.

Hobart's slate eyes followed every move. Van Hall slid from the bed, holding the microphone in his hand.

"There's an interference-free range of five hundred metres. I'm going to take a walk. The moment you hear my voice, start recording. And keep the door locked while I am gone."

Van Hall let himself out of the room. A chambermaid was piling soiled bedclothes into a laundry basket further along the corridor. She paid no attention as he walked towards the service-stairs. Once out of sight, he extended the aerial and spoke quietly into the microphone. He continued to talk for a couple of minutes and then returned to his room. Hobart opened the door. Van Hall relocked it.

"Ok, let's see what we've got."

Hobart started the tape. The recording of van Hall's voice was clear and without background noise.

Van Hall put the equipment back in the bag and closed the top.

"Let's get down to business," he said. "I want you to bug one of those conference rooms in the morning. You'll see the names on a board in the lobby. The one you're looking for is Vanteris SA. We'll only get one chance so we can't afford to screw up."

"Leave it to me," Hobart said confidently. He looked at the money van Hall gave him and pushed it into his trouser pocket.

Van Hall smiled thinly. "That's one of the things I like about you, Henry. A healthy regard for money. Call me as soon as you've located the conference room."

Hobart's room was on the second floor, facing rue Scribe. He put the bugging equipment in the cupboard and unpacked his overnight bag. He hung his two shirts and wetcombed his hair in front of the bathroom mirror. He counted the money van Hall had given him. Five hundred pounds. It was as much as he'd been earning in a month and he sensed that there was more to come. The prospect of bugging the conference room left him unmoved. He had done as much a dozen times before with less sophisticated equipment than van Hall had provided. Hobart had tried to run his own check on van Hall but had failed. There was a hint of an accent in van Hall's voice at times; other than that, the man's command of English was excellent.

Hobart slipped the microphone in his blazer pocket and left the rest of the equipment locked in the clothes closet. A lift-boy ferried him down to the lobby. The conference rooms were up on the second floor. A board on an easel gave the particulars of people who had booked the conference rooms for the following day. Vanteris SA was chalked in for Room Six at 11 A.M. Hobart walked up the wide staircase. The distinctive smell of a hairdressing salon came from a corridor on his left. Gauze curtains veiled the activities behind the plateglass windows. The six conference rooms followed in sequence. Numbers one, three and six were open. He took a quick glance towards the staircase and stepped smartly sideways, shutting the door as he went.

Number six was furnished with chairs and a table, the ashtrays and glasses were dirty, the water-carafe empty. Scribbling pads carried the hotel logo. The two heating registers were covered with fretted wood. A quick inspection showed that the casing on the registers could be removed. He took the mike from his pocket. The powerful magnet held it in place on the metal radiator. He replaced the cover and peered through the fretting. There was no sign of the mike. He opened a crack in the door, waiting for a chance to slip into the corridor unnoticed. Opportunity came within seconds. He walked back along the corridor and up to his room. The mike was voice-activated and would set the tape-recorder in motion.

He lifted the phone. "Hotel Fleur-de-Lys, Square Louvois. I don't know the number, I'm sorry."

A woman came on the line. "I'd like to speak to Mister Cameron," Hobart said.

"Mister Cameron is not here, sir."

"Can you tell me when he'll be back?"

The woman's voice conveyed disapproval. "Mister Cameron does not inform me of his movements."

"Can you take a message?" asked Hobart.

The answer came grudgingly. "If you wish."

"Tell him that Henry Hobart is in Paris for a couple of days and would like to see him. Tell him I'll be in Fat Sam's, ten o'clock tonight."

She repeated the gist of the message, running the words together in a nasal monotone. Hobart relinquished the phone. Kirk Cameron was the right man to spend an evening in Paris with. He knew the city and spoke the lingo. Hobart was usually proofed against charm in both men and women, but he made an exception in Cameron's case. Hobart had long since lost touch with his family and had no friends. It was good to be able to call someone and know that the call would be welcome.

The Fleur-de-Lys Hotel was a couple of hundred yards from the Opéra. Built in the eighteen-nineties, it had stayed as it was ever since. It was a family-run establishment with twelve bedrooms, two with bathrooms attached. The other rooms were fitted with showerstalls. Most of the tenants rented their rooms by the month.

Kirk Cameron came in from the street. He was thirty-six years old, six feet and a couple of inches tall, with cropped reddish hair and a face slashed with laugh-lines. A hockey-puck traveling at seventy miles an hour had scarred his left cheekbone. He was wearing a cabbage-green corduroy suit and a checked flannel shirt. The hotel lobby was sparsely furnished. A horsehair bench, a couple of chairs and a table littered with out-of-date magazines left by transient guests. The night-clerk looked up from his desk as Cameron approached.

"It's cold out there," the Canadian said in French, shivering theatrically. The sun had been shining that morning and he had left his room without a coat.

The clerk slapped a piece of paper on the counter between them. It was written in the fancy script of the proprietress.

Monsieur Hobart will be at Fat Sam's at ten o'clock tonight. Kindly settle your bill!

The clerk leaned on his elbows, waiting. He was a Marseillais whose wife had decamped with a ship's cook from Vancouver. The experience had left him with a murderous hatred of all things Canadian. Cameron's presence in the hotel was a source of constant affront to him. He straightened his back, displaying a mouthful of dental caries as he watched Cameron study the bill. Fourteen days at one hundred and fifty francs came to two thousand one hundred francs, service and tax included.

Cameron put the bill in his pocket. "I'll deal with this in the morning. Give me my key."

The clerk was clearly enjoying himself. "First pay the bill. Those are my instructions."

The blood rose on Cameron's neck. "You listen to me, my friend! My passport's up in my room and you're preventing me from getting it. That's illegal."

The clerk squinted. "Refusing to pay for your room, that's not illegal? No money, no key. That's the deal."

"You'll hear more of this," Cameron warned. The clerk lifted a stubby finger.

It seemed even colder outside. Cameron buttoned the neck of his shirt and walked down the street to the Métro. Everything he owned was up in his room, his brushes and paints, two bags of clothing and the hundred-dollar bill that he had kept for emergencies. Such work as he had produced during the last six months was in the hands of Irma Hoenigsberg, a fifty-year-old Rumanian with a picture gallery on Île Saint-Louis and a loose hold on five languages. Madame Hoenigsberg specialized in subsidizing struggling painters, taking fifty per cent at any sale that she made of their work. She kept no accounts, doing her sums in her head, doling out amounts of money from a seemingly bottomless reticule. According to her, Cameron remained permanently in her debt.

Cameron descended the steps to the warmth of the Métro.

There would be no problem in finding a bed for the night. Madame Hoenigsberg's light burned bright for favored protégés, Cameron included. She was fat, coarse and demanding. The trick was to arrive late when she was full of wine. Cameron surfaced at Pont Marie and crossed the bridge to Île Saint-Louis. Eighteenth century houses presented elegant façades to the dark, fast-flowing river. The island was a village where the inhabitants considered others as foreigners. A footbridge at the end of the street led to the floodlit glory of Notre Dame.

Cameron paused for a moment, glancing up at the second-floor windows of an apartment building. Lights showed behind drawn curtains. Irma was a woman of fixed habits. She would be up there reading Proust, her stout legs supported by a tapestry-covered stool and a glass of Côte-du-Rhône beside her. Cameron turned into a doorway under a lighted box-sign.

FAT SAM'S PIANO BAR

Cameron walked down the stairs to what had once been a cellar. The mahogany bar dwarfed five empty tables. There was an upright piano with the top removed. The still life hanging on the white-washed wall had been painted by Cameron and accepted as payment for a three-month bar-bill. Fat Sam opened his bar at ten o'clock, closing it with the exit of the last customer. He was a Trinidadian negro whose sweetness of nature had survived eighteen years in Paris. He held out both arms in welcome. His smile split his face horizontally.

"How you doing, my man?"

"I've been a whole lot better," said Cameron. "Give me a beer," he said to the Vietnamese girl behind the bar.

She took a bottle from the cooler and placed it in front of him.

"I've just been thrown out of my room," he proclaimed. "The bastards tossed me out on the street. Everything I own is there." He felt in his pocket for money.

"That drink on me," said Fat Sam, propping his belly against the brass rail. "What about Irma, you sleeping she house tonight?"

Cameron's shrug indicated his hopelessness.

"That woman thief you, man," said Fat Sam. "This go teach you a lesson."

Cameron emptied his glass. "She's no worse than the rest of them. Give me another beer."

This time it was Fat Sam who went to the cooler. He wiped the neck of the bottle, clearly disposed to continue the conversation.

"Use the brain God give you," he said. "Truth have to be said between friends. You is a good painter, Kirk. Why you think I pay you three thousand francs for that?" He pointed to the still life on the wall.

"Eight hundred," Cameron corrected. "I asked for a thousand to pay the bar-bill. You gave me two hundred change. I spent it in here."

A look of pain spread across Fat Sam's face. "I swear I worry you ever take up with that woman. She no good for you, man. I don't know what is get into you!"

"Try painting instead of playing piano and you'll have the answer," said Cameron. "Fifty per cent of something's worth a lot more than one hundred per cent of nothing."

He turned his head to see Henry Hobart coming down the stairs, his long black raincoat slung around his shoulders like a cloak. His eyes roved round the room and settled on Cameron. Hobart pointed a finger, grinning.

"Let's have a couple of slammers here," he told the bar-girl. He was wearing highwaisted trousers and a blazer with brass buttons beneath his raincoat. His pale hair was brushed flat. Cameron and Hobart sat down at a table facing one another. The Vietnamese girl carried a tray across laden with bottles and two glasses. She half-filled the glasses with tequila, added champagne to the first glass and placed a cloth on top of it. She raised the glass and slammed it down hard on the table. She whipped off the cloth and handed the foaming drink to Cameron. The mixture exploded in his brain. She did the same with the second glass. Hobart wiped his mouth with the back of his hand.

"Only a few of us left, mate!"

Fat Sam had introduced the *rápido* to Hobart, who saw it as his own invention. The Englishman belched.

"So tell me," he said. "What have you been up to since we last met?"

As far as Cameron was concerned, Hobart was an amiable enough individual with a string of anecdotes colored by Raymond Chandler. They had met the previous year in the bar.

"You're looking at a man with a problem," said Cameron.

Fat Sam spoke like a man from the tomb. "I go tell you his problem," he said. He pointed at the still-life again. "Look at them colors. Look at them apple and pear fruit! That painting worth a lot of money, I tell you. This bitch thief Kirk's just rewards. Just look at he face. He walking the streets this very night."

"Why don't you play some music," said Cameron.

The Trinidadian liked playing even more than talking. He hitched a reinforced stool under his heavy behind and sat down at the keyboard. He hit a couple of chords and went into an E-flat rendition of "Southbound Blues." His voice was lemon-and-honey. Once launched he was deaf to everything except the music.

"What the hell's he talking about?" Hobart asked.

Cameron's shoulders rose and fell. "They locked me out of my room. I'm surprised the old bag even gave me your message."

Hobart stared hard. He had clearly been drinking. "How do you mean, locked you out of your room?"

Cameron dropped the hotel bill on the table between them. "I don't have the money to pay it, it's as simple as that."

Hobart's lips moved as he added the figures. He signaled the girl.

"Two more *rápidos,*" he ordered. He produced a roll of hundred-franc notes from an inside pocket. He peeled off twenty-five and pushed them across the table. "Don't take offense," he said. "There's enough to pay the bill and eat for a couple of days. You can pay me back when you've got it."

Cameron fingered the money with disbelief. "You're serious?"

"About money I'm always serious," Hobart said. "This woman who's handling your paintings, can't you get rid of her?"

"Not really. She's got everything I've painted during the last six months."

"So paint some more," Hobart said. "You've still got the studio."

"Yep!" Cameron said. The lie came easily. Irma Hoenigsberg paid half the rent of the Marais studio that Cameron shared. The truth was that Cameron had been eating on the rent for the last three weeks.

The girl banged the glasses again. "Put the money away," Hobart said. "I'm rich at the moment."

Cameron's drink tasted even better the second time round. The pianist changed key, sliding into "Stormy Weather," one of the Canadian's favorites. High heels clicked down the stairs. Two women came into the bar. The taller was a Pole with the features of a Baltic aristocrat and a cap of gleaming black hair. She was wearing a velvet trouser suit and trailing a red fox jacket. Her companion was a blonde ikon dealer from Auteuil, her face partly concealed behind the upturned collar of her camelhair coat. Fat Sam continued to play as each woman kissed his cheek in turn. Both waved at Cameron.

"They're friends of Irma's," said Cameron. "And don't get ideas. They're a couple."

Hobart belched again. "What a waste."

"That's life," said Cameron. A feeling of well-being had arrived with the second slammer. "So what brings you to Paris?"

Hobart looked sly. "I'm getting paid a lot of money for a specialist job."

"Why not?" said Cameron. He was accustomed to the Englishman's bragging. The fact remained that Hobart had just given him twenty-five hundred francs.

Hobart dragged his eyes from the women and lowered his voice.

"Industrial espionage," he whispered hoarsely.

Cameron nodded as though he understood.

Hobart placed a finger against his lips. "I can't say more. What are we going to do now?"

Cameron shifted uneasily. "I thought I'd get back and pay the bill. That way I'm sure of my bed."

"There's no food here and I'm hungry," said Hobart. "I haven't eaten since breakfast. I'm not talking about a late one, just something to eat and then home. I've got the cash." He patted his inside pocket.

"Ok," said Cameron, pushing his chair back. He aimed a fist at the pianist. "We're going to split, Sam. I'll catch you later."

Fat Sam crashed a chord in response. Hobart placed some money on the bar and they left. They waited on the corner until a cab cruised up. The driver was one of the old school, leather coat and greasy beret and no interest in unnecessary dialogue. He sat with the motor running. His life was no more than one long skirmish with the public.

"Mishka's, rue du Four," Cameron told him. "You like Russian food?" he asked Hobart as they leaned back against the upholstery.

The Englishman turned his hand up and over. "I don't eat that much of it."

"You're in for a treat," Cameron assured him.

They pushed through the thick felt curtains that shielded the restaurant entrance. The babble was loud inside. It was difficult to see through the haze of cigarette-smoke. Young people dressed as waiters and waitresses scooted about, balancing trays. There was an empty table near the swing door that led to the kitchen. The débris left by the previous guests was still on the boldly striped cloth. A girl wearing a checked apron pushed a menu into Cameron's hand and plucked a pencil from her shingled hair. Cameron ignored the bill-of-fare.

"We'll take the piroshki," he ordered. "Followed by shashlik and sweet pancakes."

She whipped off the candlestick and put it down on the floor. Then she gathered the tablecloth by its four corners. Plates, ashtrays and cutlery dropped to the bottom of the bundle. She fired bundle and contents through the swing door, placed fresh table-settings and restored the candlestick to its original position. She touched a match to it.

"What would you gentlemen like to drink?" Her accent was East Coast American.

"Stolichnaya," said Cameron.

She dropped a quick curtsey and vanished. Hobart jammed both elbows on the table and stared after her.

"What was all that about?"

"These kids are students," said Cameron. "You don't come here for the service."

The piroshki was served with a spiced ground meat filling, the lamb on a flaming spit. The pancakes were topped with sour cream and honey. The vodka bottle was encased in ice. Cameron took a pick to it. They drank from small glasses and ate slowly. Hobart still belching. Done with his meal, it seemed important to him that he explained himself.

"A lot of cowboys in our business," he said, reaching for a

toothpick. "The public don't know the half of it. Take those advertisements you see in the newspapers. 'Confidential enquiries undertaken.' Let me tell you what that means. It means standing in someone's back garden, rain running down your fucking neck, waiting for some bastard built like Mike Tyson to come down and put your chin through the top of your head."

He rapped himself hard on the chest and looked at the tablecloth as though in a state of suspended animation. He finished the last of his vodka.

"Not me," he said, winking. "I can walk into any office in the City of London. I'm respected. They know who they're dealing with. I could tell you stories that would make your hair stand on end."

Cameron pushed the bill in Hobart's direction. "I'll take you back to your hotel."

Hobart came to his feet unsteadily and wrapped himself in his long black raincoat.

"I'm all right. I'll drop you off."

The entrance to the Fleur-de-Lys was shut tight, nobody at the desk. Cameron opened the cab-door.

"Thanks for everything, Henry. Look me up when you're in Paris again. I won't forget what you've done for me."

Hobart lurched at Cameron's sleeve. "I can tell what a man's made of by looking him in the eye. You're okay."

Cameron freed himself. "Get some sleep, Henry, we'll see one another." He closed the cab door.

"I'll call you before I leave," Hobart shouted.

Cameron leaned on the night-bell. A dog yapped inside the hotel. It was some time before the clerk came into view, tousled and wearing a scarf round his neck. He moved with the speed of a man on his way to his execution. He unfastened the door and dragged it back as far as the chain allowed.

"Get out of here," he snarled, "or I'll call the police."

Cameron displayed a handful of hundred-franc notes. The door opened slowly.

"I want a receipt," Cameron warned, offering the bill and the money.

The clerk counted the cash. Black stubble sprouted from his cheeks and he was clearly in a state of some disturbance.

Cameron reached across and took his room-key from the board.

"And there's another thing. You've got a lethal case of halitosis. Either you get it seen to or I'll have to report you to the World Health Organization."

The telephone rang, drilling straight into Hobart's dreamless stupor. He reached for the bedside table. The call came from the switchboard.

"It is precisely seven hours and forty-five minutes, Sir!"

Movement sent splinters of glass deep into Hobart's eyeballs.

"Tell room-service to bring me a pot of coffee and some Vitamin C," he said and lay back on the pillows.

Seven forty-five. He was still well ahead of schedule. He rolled out of bed and stood in front of the open window, gulping in air. A waiter from room-service knocked on the door. Hobart drained the foaming Alka-Seltzer and cradled the coffee cup in shaking hands. Life returned to his veins reluctantly. He counted the money on the dressing table. A little more than one hundred of the five hundred pounds van Hall had given him was left. Memory provided details of the previous night. He had no regret about paying Cameron's hotel bill. Being the Canadian's benefactor gave Hobart a sense of superiority.

It was half-past nine by the time he went down to the lobby. People were crowding around the Reception Desk, checking in or out. Hobart dropped onto a couch with a copy of the *Daily Mail*. He had a clear view of the staircase from where he sat. He read through the newspaper and attempted the crossword. At a quarter-to-eleven he walked up to the second floor and loitered in front of the hair-dressing salon. All the conference rooms were already occupied with the exception of Number Six. That door was still open. Doubt nibbled away at his confidence. Given the right equipment it was easy to ascertain if a room was bugged. Maybe they ran a security check every morning. He slipped into the room and examined the heating register. The microphone was still in place. As he started walking back along the corridor, two men came from the staircase. The taller was wearing a tweed suit with leather patches on the elbows of the jacket. He was about forty years old with thick brown hair. His right eye was made of glass. His companion was five or six years younger with Hispanic features. The two men were talking in Spanish. Neither glanced his way as they passed. Hobart hurried upstairs to his room. He hung a DO NOT DISTURB sign on his door and unlocked the clothes-closet. He put the tape-recording unit on the bed. The spools were already turning. He found a chair, a sense of repose supporting his roving thoughts. Van Hall represented the break-through he had always hoped for. He saw himself installed in an office with a long-legged blonde as his secretary. Clients—he liked the word—would arrive, sent by van Hall. There'd be missions to far-off places. He'd take no more divorce work or skiptracing, nothing but industrial espionage. He thought of himself as being informed in a world of uninstructed idiots. The tape stopped, jerking him back to reality. He played it back one more time, understanding nothing but making sure that there was no break in transmission. He returned the electronic equipment to its case and lifted the phone. Van Hall answered.

"I've got it," said Hobart. It was hard to control his excitement.

"Okay," said van Hall. He might have been talking to the milk-man. "Bring it over right away."

Van Hall put the phone back in its cradle. There was no sure way of knowing what would be on the tape but he had faith in Mesquita's information. The Doctor always gave value. Van Hall reasoned that although he had done many illegal things in his life, this required careful thought. He had no intention of putting himself in danger. The secret of being a successful scoundrel was paying someone else to take the risk. He had made up his mind about Hobart some time ago. No game was straight for the man unless it was crooked. Larceny was embedded deep in Hobart's heart. The trick was to tell him no more than he needed to know.

A tap came on the door. It was the enquiry agent carrying the electronic case in one hand, his long black raincoat in the other. He put the bag on the bed and sat down beside it. His shirt collar was open, his chin flecked with dried blood.

"God Almighty," said van Hall, shaking his head. "What time did you get to bed?"

Hobart turned away from his mirrored reflection. "What dif-ference as long as I got the job done?"

Van Hall sprang the locks on the bag. "Wasting your money on whores, I suppose."

"Wrong," Hobart said. "An evening of culture with a painter friend."

Van Hall set the tape in motion. "Have you played this?"

"Yep," Hobart said. He took the half-empty bottle of Perrier from the bedside table, drank greedily and wiped his mouth on his handkerchief. "Sounds as clear as a bell, not that I understood a word of it. The Spanish guy sounded as if he was popping a blood vessel."

Van Hall kept his voice casual. "Did you see either of them?"

"Saw them both," Hobart said. "They came up the stairs together. I passed them in the corridor. The Spanish is about thirty-five, -six, sharp dresser and medium height. The other geezer's a few years older with a glass eye. He's wearing a tweed suit with the leather patches on the elbows. One of the Signet-ring-on-the-little-finger brigade."

Van Hall cocked his head. "For someone who just happened to be passing by, you seem to have noticed a great deal."

"That's what you pay me for." Hobart leaned back against the headboard and closed his eyes.

The tape-machine clicked a few times, then the dialogue began. The first voice was Ortega's, his Spanish a rattle of accusation.

"This meeting is both imprudent and pointless, Señor!"

The Englishman's voice was slower. "I have called you from London on five different occasions. Each time you have been evasive. This matter has to be settled once and for all."

"As far as we are concerned the matter *is* settled!" Ortega retorted. "You were paid the sum we agreed on."

"Half," Sheffield said. "The balance is still outstanding."

Ortega made a sound of impatience. "Your mission was unsuccessful."

"Your godfather allowed my men to walk into a trap. They were shot down like dogs."

Something scraped across the surface of the conference room table, an ashtray or a glass.

"The General is not to blame," Ortega said. "It was Pinochet's idea to order a decoy-car for the return to the capital. A chance whim—who knows? In any case there was no way of contacting your people. Nobody knew where they were. The whole affair is deeply regrettable."

"Your instructions were filled to the letter," Sheffield argued.

"You are evading the issue," said Ortega. "My godfather had no knowledge of the decoy-car until it joined the motorcade at Cho-caltapa."

Sheffield spoke more slowly than the other man but no less forcefully. "I have told you repeatedly. I am not concerned with you or your godfather. You take good care of yourselves. My concern is with the families of the four men who died, their dependents. Mercenaries carry no life insurance. I want the rest of the money that was promised."

Ortega's voice was starched and arrogant. "You are wasting your time, Señor Sheffield. I have already discussed this with the General. He is adamant. Whatever you hear me say is what he says. I am sorry."

Sheffield made a sound in his throat. "I had a visitor a few days ago. He came to my house unannounced, late at night. He had all the right credentials. He made the purpose of his visit very clear. Approval of the security forces does not extend to failure. Do I make myself clear?"

"No." The answer was uncompromising.

"They make no secret of it," said Sheffield. "These people are not concerned about you or me or your godfather. They are concerned about the credibility of Her Majesty's Government. They want this whole matter closed, no scandals, no international incidents."

"In that case, what are we doing here?"

"We are here to make sure that your godfather honors his word," Sheffield said. "I want the rest of the money you promised, five hundred thousand pounds to be distributed among the dependents of the four dead men."

"I have already told you, you are wasting your time. The General will not change his mind."

"Let me try to help him," Sheffield said. "I have a safety-deposit box in London. In it are copies of my invoice to you and your check in my favor drawn on the Banque Ottomane."

There was a long pause before Ortega answered. "I do not take kindly to threats."

Sheffield continued. "If necessary I am ready to swear an affidavit setting out the details of your part and your godfather's part in this affair. Details of the weaponry involved, dates and addresses."

"This is blackmail," Ortega said.

"Insurance," Sheffield corrected. "It is necessary in my line of business. People requiring my services are rarely honorable. Think about it, Señor Ortega. Talk with your godfather. I am flying to Rome tonight. I will be back in London the day after tomorrow. You have my home number. Call me there. I shall be expecting an answer."

Ortega's voice thickened with rage. "You are making a grave mistake. You are in no position to blackmail me."

Sheffield sounded unmoved. "I have committed no offense against my country. I never expected my business to last forever. This is a matter of principle, Señor Ortega. Even you should be able to understand that."

Ortega was shouting now. "I will destroy you!"

"It would be wiser to defend your godfather. I shall expect your telephone call the day after tomorrow."

Chairs were scraped back and the tape stopped. Hobart opened his eyes and yawned.

"I hope you got your money's worth."

Van Hall removed the cassette and dropped it in his pocket.

"What time does your plane leave?"

Hobart shook himself out of his stupor. "Nineteen hours twenty."

"That Englishman you saw this morning. Would you recognize him again?"

Hobart's small eyes opened wider. "I'd know them both, no problem."

"We're only interested in the one at the moment. His name is Paul Sheffield and he runs an outfit called Cyclops Security."

A hoover droned along the corridor. Van Hall made sure that the door was shut properly.

"You ever hear of Cyclops?" he asked.

Hobart shook his head.

"Sheffield is ex-SAS," van Hall said. "So are the people who work for him. And don't let the glass eye fool you. He saw you as well, you can bet on it."

Hobart's pale blue gaze retreated into his eye-sockets. "Nobody saw me go into that conference room, *or* come out of it. That much I'm sure about."

Van Hall removed his back from the door. "Know your problem, Henry? You're the kind of guy when he leaves, his hostess starts counting the spoons. The correct word is 'dubious.' You've been pulling cheap stunts all your life. No imagination."

Hobart's face colored. "Imagination's no good if you don't get the chance to use it."

A pigeon flew off the windowledge, leaving a feather behind.

"Suppose I *give* you the chance," said van Hall. "How would you like to earn a great deal of money? Enough to let you do whatever it is you dream about up in that garret."

Hobart took another swig from the Perrier bottle. "Who do I have to kill?"

"No-one." Van Hall was smiling. "Just a little light larceny."

Hobart's fingers were shaking as he lit a cigarette. "You are talking about my speciality. God knows it would pay better than what I've been doing."

Van Hall gave him a slip of paper. "Memorize that and destroy it."

Hobart scanned the name and address. "Paul Sheffield, three hundred and six Holland Park." He tore the paper in shreds.

"You'll find his phone number in the book," said van Hall. "The place is empty until the day after tomorrow. I want you to get in there sometime tonight. Burgle the place. It's important that nobody knows that you've been there. Do you think you could handle that, Henry?"

Hobart removed a speck of lint from his sleeve. "What am I supposed to be stealing?"

"Nothing," van Hall replied. "You don't take as much as a match. Get that firmly inside your head. All you do is use your eyes. I want you to look wherever a man keeps papers. Sheffield rents a safety-deposit box. I need to know where it is. You might find a bill, correspondence of some kind."

"What about a burglar-alarm?"

"I've no idea," said van Hall. "Why, does that bother you?"

Hobart shook his head. "No. Someone comes to me, wants to know what's going on in some private premises, and there's an alarm fitted, that doesn't stop me. All I do is ask for more money."

"Never mind the money," said van Hall. "Are you sure you can handle it without leaving traces behind?"

"Certain." Hobart spoke with confidence.

"There's something we'd better discuss at this stage," said van Hall. "There can be no going back. Once you're in, you're in."

Hobart lifted his chin. "I've known you over three years now, Mister van Hall. You've always been straight with me. I've always been straight with you. That's the way I'd like to keep it."

Van Hall smiled. "Of course. Otherwise it would be like committing suicide."

The thought seemed to have impact. It was a while before Hobart spoke again.

"You spoke about money. What would be in it for me?"

Van Hall turned from the window. "Let me explain something to you. This is going to be serious business, a carefully planned venture with fail-safe devices. It'll be done in two stages. Getting into Sheffield's place is the first. I'm pretty sure that you'll find what we need. You'll get a thousand pounds cash in your hand. That's when we move into the second phase. You're looking at a hundred thousand pounds for your end, Henry."

Hobart's lips moved soundlessly. He reached across and shook van Hall's hand.

"You can count me in. If what you want is in Sheffield's place, be sure that I'll find it."

"I think you will," van Hall said, smiling. "Now we come to another matter. We'll need another man for the second phase of our operation. Someone who won't ask questions. No villains, that's important. The man's got to be able to drive and have a clean license."

"Why is he going to be driving?"

Van Hall moved his forefinger from side to side. "It's why he *thinks* he's going to be driving that matters, Henry. I'll leave that to you. You could tell him it's one of your professional jobs, perhaps. Do you know anyone likely?"

Hobart was bubbling. "Couldn't have come at a better time. This Canadian I was with last night, the painter. He's skint. I had to pay his hotel bill. He's one of those happygolucky guys and he doesn't know shit from shortbread. The thing is, he believes whatever I tell him. He's never even been to the U.K."

"Let's get one thing straight, though. I don't want to see the man nor do you mention my name to him."

"Understood," Hobart said.

"When can you get hold of him?"

Hobart turned his wrist and consulted his watch. "I'm supposed to be having lunch with him as it happens."

"Do it," said van Hall, and opened his wallet. "Here's another five hundred pounds and three for expenses. Tell your friend what you like. I don't want any slip-ups. Call me when you've talked with him and take the bag back to London with you."

Hobart picked up the bag with the electronic equipment in it. The door closed behind him.

The café was on a corner, a hundred yards down the street from Cameron's hotel. Hobart paid off the cab. His baggage was already at the airline terminal. Cameron was sitting at a window-table, reading the *Herald-Tribune*. He was wearing the green corduroy suit, a shirt with a buttondown collar and elastic-sided chukka boots. He pulled out a chair for Hobart.

Hobart sat down, wincing. "Why don't you suffer?"

"I'm a much nicer person," Cameron said, grinning. He ordered another coffee from the Moroccan waiter.

"We're going to have to skip lunch," announced Hobart. "Some business came up—important business—I had to change flights. I'm on the airbus at fifteen forty-five."

The Canadian folded his newspaper, a different man after a good night's rest. He wore a smile like a second skin.

"That's too bad. Ah well, there'll be other times."

Hobart pushed his coffee aside, spread his arms on the table and leaned forward confidentially.

"Did you get yourself sorted out at the hotel?"

"I paid the bill, if that's what you mean," Cameron said. "The old bag who owns the place wanted me out. I've left my stuff at Irma Hoenigsberg's gallery. I'll find a room later, no problem."

He was smoking a Ce rolled in maize paper. The smell made Hobart's head reel. He ground the butt into the ashtray.

"Have you got a driving-license?"

"I've got two, provincial and international, what makes you ask?"

Hobart leaned closer. "This lawyer I'm involved with, the one I told you about. He called me this morning. He's got a client who's having trouble with the custody of her daughter. There's a million-pound trust fund at stake. I've got the job. From what the lawyer says, it could be a tough one. I'm going to need help, are you interested?"

Cameron had pulled some matches from a box and was engaged in making them into triangles. He answered without raising his head.

"I'm a painter, not a snoop."

"You're a painter who can't pay his hotel bill," said Hobart. "All you've got to do is drive me round. This is a big one for me and I don't want to lose it. We're talking a couple of grand for a week's work."

Cameron looked up. "A couple of grand! What's the catch?"

"The woman's husband. He's a right bastard according to all accounts. I know the detective agency that's working for his lawyers and they're no better. Things could get a little bit hairy. I mean, you can take care of yourself, right?"

Cameron's smile broke again, dragging the scar on his cheekbone. "For that kind of money, I don't mind coming off second best."

"Good then, that's settled." Hobart spread five fifty-pound notes on the table. "That'll buy your ticket and leave something over for expenses. Once you're in London, find yourself a quiet hotel."

Cameron pushed the money in an inside pocket.

"You're the wrong shape for a fairy godmother, but thanks all the same. When do you want me in England?"

"Tomorrow," said Hobart. "Call me as soon as you arrive. You've got my home number. We'll be hiring a car. Don't forget your driving-license."

He shimmied into his long black raincoat. "Goodbye, then," he said.

He looked back as he passed the window. Cameron was playing with his matches again. There had to be people like that, Hobart thought. And there had to be people like van Hall. And here he was in the middle, suddenly a man of substance.

TWO

It was shortly after seven o'clock in the evening on Île Saint-Louis. The café was noisy and thick with tobacco smoke. John and Kirstie Raven were drinking Pernod. He was six feet and three inches tall with greying hair that had once been blond. His main feature was his eyes. Dark blue in color, he used them on occasion like a camera lens, focusing on his subject and closing the lids momentarily. He was wearing an old black fishing sweater and well-washed jeans. His wife's black velvet suit supplied the chic. Whisky-colored hair hung to her shoulders, and her elegant legs were crossed at the knee.

She rose without warning and walked through the door to the pavement outside. Raven had a clear view of her, holding a stranger by the hand and talking excitedly. She pulled the man back through the door into the café, still holding him by the hand. Her smile lit the room.

"See who I found!" she proclaimed to her husband. "One of my best and dearest old friends! We were at school together in Switzerland. This is Kirk Cameron, John. Kirk, meet my husband."

Raven hauled himself up and offered his hand. "Why don't you sit down and join us, Kirk? What can we get you to drink?"

"I'll take a beer." Cameron sat down between them.

Raven lifted a hand. Madame Bompard shuffled across, a small compact figure in a rusty black dress and felt slippers. She gave short shrift to drunks and hookers and ignored requests for service. For Raven she made an exception. They had first met when he had been a detective-sergeant working out of Scotland Yard and squiring his future wife. In spite of his subsequent retirement, Raven remained "Monsieur l'Inspecteur" for Madame Bompard. She took his order and bulldozed her way back to the bar.

Cameron wrapped an arm around Kirstie's waist and drew her close.

"I don't *believe* this!" He grinned at Raven. "Of all people to run into, this one!"

Raven's smile was polite. He was reminded of the boxes of photographs, souvenirs of his wife's three-year stay in the co-educational school, near Montreux. Pictures of Kirstie on skis; Kirstie on a boat on the lake; clowning in some turret window. There were more than a hundred snapshots and Cameron figured in half of them.

The Canadian was a couple of inches shorter than Raven with a rusty crewcut, a ready smile and a bonewhite scar on his left cheekbone. He was wearing a cucumber-green corduroy suit with a pink shirt and brown elastic-sided boots. His raincoat was see-through plastic. He shook his head at Raven.

"It's literally *years* since I saw her!" His arm was still around Kirstie's waist.

"Ten," Kirstie said. "Toronto. Jamie was still at Metro School of Art. We all went to that party in Cabbagetown. Remember that clown from the R.C.M.P., the one who said he'd been one of Trudeau's bodyguards? He was going to have the lot of us busted for smoking a joint."

She and Cameron grinned at the memory. Raven had not seen his wife as relaxed in months. Meeting Cameron seemed to have recharged her batteries.

"Do you live here or are you on holiday?" Raven asked.

"I live here," said Cameron. He waved vaguely. "My dealer has a gallery on the island."

"Kirk's a painter," Kirstie said quickly. "He was with my brother at art school."

Raven kept it going politely. "Are you painting at the moment?"

Cameron shook his head. "I just lost my studio. You know how it goes, you don't pay the rent, they throw you out. But that's all going to change."

"But that's *awful,*" cried Kirstie. "You must have somewhere to work, for God's sake!" Her eyes strayed in her husband's direction.

He detected the unvoiced question. They used the Quai d'Anjou apartment infrequently. Why not let Cameron benefit in their absence.

"We'll put our heads together," Kirstie said quickly.

The café was filling up with regulars. Raven knew most of them by sight. The Armenian who sold ikons and sang tenor in the choir of the Greek Orthodox Church. The lesbian from the P.T.T. Daniel, who worked in the sewers in her yellow protective clothing. The regulars recognized one another with a word or nod, a sign of solidarity among those who lived or worked on the island.

Kirstie and Cameron were deep in conversation. Raven's first impression of his wife's friend was guarded. The Canadian's cavalier attitude seemed to suggest that problems were solved in the natural course of events. It was part of what would be called his charm, Raven reasoned.

The other pair drew him back into the conversation. The Canadian's arm had moved from Kirstie's waist to her shoulder.

"I didn't even know that she'd married until the year before last. Then somebody told me she'd got hitched to this Englishman, a cop."

"That was me," Raven said, smiling.

"I take it you're not still sleuthing?" asked Cameron.

"He retired," Kirstie said quickly. "He's writing a book about all his derring-do."

Raven's laugh was weaker than those of the other two. "Was she always like this?" he demanded.

The Canadian pushed his beer aside. "I'll tell you," he said. "They had this custom at school. The beginning of each term Professor Frascati would dip into a couple of hats. He'd take a guy's name from one, a girl's from the other. Whoever you drew was your official date for the rest of the term. You know, school dances, concerts and so forth. The guys used to do a lot of trading-off. You got stuck with somebody difficult, you had to pay to get her off your back. Five dollars was a lot of money in those days but it wasn't enough to get rid of Kirstie. With her you had problems. I was the only guy who wanted her."

"Chauvinist pigs, the lot of you," Kirstie said.

Her glance put Raven in mind of his manners. "Why don't you eat with us if you're not doing anything else?" he asked.

"We live just around the corner," said Kirstie. "Jamie's old apartment."

"I'd like that a lot," Cameron said. He looked from one to the other. "If you're sure it's not putting you out."

Raven rose to his feet. "Fine," he said, and lifted a hand at Madame Bompard. "Let's get out of here."

The apartment was only a hundred yards away. The pavement narrowed once they had turned the corner. There was only room for two people to walk side by side. Raven followed behind his wife and Cameron. Kirstie's brother had bought what had been a garret fourteen years before. Working with an Italian mason he burst through the ceiling into the enormous loft. Four months hard labor, humping sacks of cement and lengths of timber, transformed the garret into an apartment with double-height space. A wooden ladder connected the two levels. Kitchen and dining room were on the lower floor. Upstairs were the studio-bedrooms and bathroom. One vast window faced south, jutting out from the slate roof like the bridge on an ocean liner. The other people living in the building included an octogenarian member of the French Academy, an Italian film producer and a number of actors and actresses. Each had signed a waiver agreeing to the rape of the communal loft.

The concierge eyed them through a slit in her curtains as they crossed the courtyard. She was another of Raven's unlikely admirers. The fact that she was a known police informer had something to do with it. She was in the habit of beckoning Raven into her quarters with a great show of secrecy and relating details of the actresses's sex lives. Raven was obliged to show interest. When Madame Goujon was displeased, mail had a habit of going astray.

The trio climbed the seventy-five steps to the top floor. Cameron placed a hand against the wall and breathed hard.

"Only your friends come to visit you twice," he said, feigning dizziness.

"It's worse when you're drunk," Raven said, putting the key in the lock. The door opened directly into the dining room. Ikons glowed on the whitewashed walls. The refectory table had never been touched by furniture polish. Candle-grease and vigorous use of a dry scrubbing brush had produced a patina that reflected the light from the taper in Raven's hand.

Kirstie went up the ladder. The candles below were lit.

"Up here!" Kirstie called.

Cameron followed her. Raven went through to the kitchen. Kirstie's dead brother had been obsessed with giraffes and the Arctic. Sketches of seals with eyes like opera-singers and cows contemplating an African moon had been painted on the kitchen walls in acrylic. A lone figure wrapped in furs squatted by a blowhole cut in an affinity of ice. With the exception of a few paintings that Kirstie had retained, all her brother's work had been sold at a posthumous exhibition.

Raven opened the refrigerator and busied himself opening oysters. He covered the half-shells with shaved ice and dealt with the salmon. He wrapped three pieces of fish in aluminum foil with lemon-juice, butter and bay leaves and placed them in a slow oven. He put bread on the table, a bottle of blanc-de-blanc and the longstemmed glasses that had come from Kirstie's mother. He joined the others upstairs. The bed was eight feet square and curtained with cardinal red velvet. The counterpane was a blaze of Thai silk. Kirstie and Cameron were sitting on the end of the bed looking out through the enormous window. Rain tapped on the panes. Light from the street lamps below stretched across the wet pavements.

The unvarnished wooden floor was strewn with Afghan mats. Books and magazines were piled haphazardly. A photograph of an old man in a doorway stood on an easel, Kirstie's winning entry for the Prix Blondin.

"Guess what," she said brightly. "Kirk's coming to London tomorrow. Isn't that exciting?"

Dust from past centuries filtered down through the rafters, dis-

lodged by some passing vehicle. Raven brushed at his trouserleg
and kept quiet.

"I said Kirk's coming to London tomorrow," she repeated.

"I heard you," said Raven. "Good."

"Just a few days on business," the Canadian elaborated.

Kirstie trailed her fingers over the bedspread, leaning back and
looking at her husband.

"I told him he must stay on the boat."

"Why not?" Raven said. It was the best he could do. He managed a smile and repeated himself. "Why not, indeed?"

"It'll be much appreciated," Cameron said. He turned on the
boyish charm. "I'll try to stay out of your hair."

"Good, then," said Kirstie, "that's settled." She dragged the
curtain across the window. "He gets in about lunch time. I'll pick
him up at Heathrow."

Raven's smile was beginning to make his face muscles ache.
They ate with the dining room curtains wide open. The lights on
the opposite side of the river were blurred by the rain. It was ten
o'clock when Cameron consulted his watch.

"I have to go," he announced. "I've got to see my dealer before
she goes to bed. I enjoyed my evening very much. Thank you
both."

Raven vanished into the kitchen. He heard the front door open
and close, Kirstie's slow progress towards the kitchen. She stood
in the doorway.

"What a creep you can be at times!" she said bitterly.

Raven piled the dirty dishes on the sink-board. "Exactly how
did it manifest itself tonight, may I ask?"

His wife shook her head slowly, a puzzled look on her face. "I
do *not* understand you, John. What in hell is it, jealousy or what?"

"*Jealousy?*" he repeated. His laugh sounded false to his ears. "I
wasn't aware that I had any reason to be jealous."

"You don't," she replied. "That's the whole point. Stop acting
like an idiot."

He was suddenly aware of his age, of thinning hair and vari-
cose veins that still troubled him.

His wife was not disposed to let the subject alone.

"I wouldn't be at all surprised if Kirk doesn't find somewhere
else to stay. You made it fairly plain that he'd only be on the boat
under sufferance."

He wiped his hands on the towel and placed it back on the rail, then he turned.

"Bullshit!" he said. "Your friend's a lot thicker-skinned than you think. You do the washing-up. I'm going to bed."

THREE

Henry Hobart stepped away from the mirror. He was wearing the drab grey suit he had bought in a Fulham Road thrift-shop and his pale hair was brushed flat with a side parting. He thought of himself as a man who could leave a group of four people and neither be missed nor remembered. His first job for van Hall had been disappointing. It was a routine matter of following someone from the Citinational Bank to the Royal Automobile Club. It was some time before he caught on that each time van Hall employed him it was as a test of his moral scruples. Paris had finally proved it. He admired van Hall's style, the mixture of cunning and sophistication. Above all, he had the feeling that van Hall was the man he'd been waiting for all his life. The man who would finally appreciate his nerve and talents.

He had left home at the age of sixteen to join the *Queen of Bermuda* as an apprentice cook. The first port of call was Durban. Hobart jumped ship and made his way up to Johannesburg. Ten years later he was back in the United Kingdom and doing business as a private investigator (Lic.Fed.Inst.Crim). He worked from his home in South Kensington, a one-room apartment at the top of the house. His window overlooked the slate roofs of the born-again mews below. There was a night-time view of the floodlit Victoria and Albert Museum. His shelves contained a comprehensive collection of reference books, all stolen from public libraries. Hobart knew the law better than most laymen. His knowledge of villainy was even more extensive. It was time to produce a new image for his patron. A man who was both cool and skilful.

He donned his long black raincoat and carried the tape-recording case down the street. The humpbacked Volkswagen glistened under the drizzle. He drove half-a-mile south and parked on Flood Street, leaving an AUXILIARY AMBULANCE SERVICE card stuck in the windshield. He made his way to the Chelsea Public Library. Van Hall was waiting on a bench under a window. He was wearing a dark blue vicuna overcoat with a velvet collar. He put his newspaper down and made room on the bench for Hobart.

"I had a look at the place last night," Hobart said. "It's belled."

Van Hall smoothed his neck with his fingers. "I thought you could deal with that."

"I can." Hobart put the tape-recorder bag at the other man's feet. "I'm going back there tonight. You want me to call you as soon as I'm through?"

Van Hall rose, collecting the bag on the floor. "Just stay away from the phone. What you do is come straight to this address." He gave Hobart a slip of paper and left.

Hobart watched him out-of-sight and walked back to the parked Volkswagen. He smoothed the piece of paper with his fingers.

The address van Hall had given him was near Regent's Park. He drove half-a-mile in the drizzle before he found a place to park near Onslow Gardens. He propped the ambulance card on the dashboard and took some keys from the glove compartment. He hurried back to number thirty-eight. The basement flat in his building had been empty for two years. It was damp, dark and cold in winter. The managing agents had deleted it from their list of properties for rent. Nobody had noticed Hobart's stealthy intrusion.

He descended the steps now and opened the heavy door at the bottom. The place was in darkness. There was neither power, gas nor water. He picked the flash-lamp up from the floor and lit his way along the cobwebbed passage to the room at the rear of the house. The windows were tightly shuttered. Hobart had discov-

ered the old standfree safe on his first reconnaissance. It had been
open with the key in the lock. Since then he had used it to store
what he called his work tools, a collection of skeleton keys,
lockpicks and files. There was also a wooden box full of uniforms.
The Saint John's Ambulance Brigade was his favorite. It rarely
failed to get him past security.

He climbed the inside stairs and stood with an ear to the door
at the top. There was no sound of movement beyond. He let
himself into the hallway. Most of the other tenants had nine-to-
five jobs. Hobart steered clear of them. He picked up a buff envelope on the hallway table. It was addressed to THE OCCUPANT FLAT
13 38 ONSLOW GARDENS SW7 (If undelivered return to the Electoral
Officer Town Hall Honiton Street W8).

Hobart shredded the envelope and contents on his way up the
stairs. He did his best to stay outside the system, paying cash to
doctors and dentists rather than be enmeshed in the National
Health Service. As far as he knew, the National Police Computer
had no knowledge of him. He unlocked his flat, closed the curtains and stretched out on the bed, thinking about his visit to
Sheffield's home. He set his alarm for six o'clock and slept.
Awake, he returned to the basement unnoticed by any of the
other tenants. He changed into overalls and heavy work boots. A
duffelcoat completed his outfit. He made certain he carried nothing that bore his name and address. He pulled a plastic-covered
identity card from the box. It had been issued by the London
Electricity Board to someone called Walter Thread. Hobart's photograph replaced the original. He left the building by the basement steps, carrying his toolbox. He hurried through the rain to
the Volkswagen, removed the card from the windshield and put
it in the glove-compartment.

It was twenty minutes past seven when he turned the small car
up the rise from Bayswater Road. Sheffield's house was at the top
of the hill facing the entrance to Holland Park. The park gates
were shut. Sheffield lived in a two-storey Regency replica set between two larger homes. Hobart slackened speed as he passed. A
light burned in Sheffield's hallway, two more on the upper floor.
Experience told him that the lights would be time-switched. The
burglar-alarm was more dangerous. Sheffield's neighbors might
know of his absence—the alarm could be wired to the police station. Hobart parked between streetlamps, left the car keys in the

tail-pipe and walked down the hill, toolbox under his arm. Three
iron covers were set in the pavement in front of Sheffield's house.
One belonged to the water-board, the second to British Telecom.
Hobart squatted in front of the third and lifted the lid of his box.
He fitted a pair of steel hooks into the slots on the iron cover and
straightened his back. The solid slab was heavier than he had
expected. Rain ran down his neck. The cavity was lined with
brick. A printed notice carried the warning DANGER HIGH VOLTAGE
under a skull and crossbones. Hobart threw the switch in the
junction box. The lights went out in Sheffield's house. Hobart
replaced the cover and opened the gate to the short pathway. He
put the work box under a rhododendron bush and stood by the
wall. The loss of power in Sheffield's home seemed unnoticed by
either of his neighbors. He had checked the locks on the street
door on the previous evening. He stood close, the two keys in his
gloved fingers. The first lock turned off easily. He tried five skeleton keys before finding the right fit for the Chubb mortise. He
pushed the door gently and stepped into the darkened hallway.
The noise in his eardrums was the thud of his heart. The door
clicked shut. He held the pencil-flash between his teeth and followed its narrow beam across the hallway into a room on his
right. The mirror reflected a striped satin chaise-longue in front
of a Chinese firescreen. A glass-topped table bore a box of candied
fruit and a ball-bearing toy enclosed in clear plastic. Magazines
lay on the rack underneath. The beam from the flashlight in his
mouth swung as he turned his head. Against the wall and reaching halfway to the ceiling stood a walnut escritoire. It held eight
drawers, four on each side of a polished slab of wood that lowered
on jointed brass arms, four deeper drawers below. Behind the
writing surface was a deep open recess, full of papers that appeared to have been thrown in haphazardly. Hobart drew out a
handful at random—theater programmes, unopened circulars,
begging letters from charities. He was halfway through the pile
in his hand when he saw the heading HANS SECURITY VAULTS. The
receipted account was in respect of a year's rental for a locker.
The account had been sent to William Wilberforce and dated the
previous month. He replaced the papers with the delicacy of a
surgeon. It was difficult to believe his good fortune. He had been
prepared to search the house thoroughly, the thought of failure
ever in his mind. And here he was with the job done, five minutes

after stepping into the place. It took him two minutes more to close the house and throw the switch back. The lights in Sheffield's house came on again.

The address van Hall had given him was of a small block of flats on the south side of Regent's Park. He could see the lobby through the glass entrance doors. He rang one of the bell-pushes. The street door was released. Van Hall was standing at another door in the hallway. Hobart followed him into the flat. There was a stale smell compounded of flyspray and unopened windows. The furniture in the room was shabby genteel and bore signs of wear. There was a television set and a few bad prints on the walls. Hobart had seen a hundred places like it, short rental homes for transient guests. The heating appeared to be off. Van Hall was wearing his overcoat.

Hobart unfastened the toggles on his duffelcoat and took a seat on the sagging couch. It was impossible to conceal the note of triumph in his voice.

"Hans Security Vaults, Sloane Street. Locker number two hundred and twenty."

"Tell me about it," van Hall invited.

"In a desk," Hobart said, enjoying himself. "The first place I looked, would you believe! My business, you get a nose for these things." He rendered a dramatic version of his exploits in dealing with the burglar-alarm.

Van Hall was standing at a window, looking out at Hobart's Volkswagen. His mind seemed to be on other things.

"Cameron got in," Hobart said. "He called from Heathrow. He's staying with some people over in Chelsea."

Van Hall turned, frowning. "I thought you were going to put him into a hotel."

Hobart shrugged. "He met these people in Paris. He was at school with the woman."

Van Hall pulled out a diary. "Have you got the address?"

"It's one of those houseboats down on the river, the *Albatross*. The name of the people is Raven."

Van Hall scribbled and closed his diary. "What have you told him?"

Hobart leaned back. "I gave him this story about a job I've got from a lawyer acting for a rich woman with a husband who's suing for divorce. The husband's hired some ex-cop who's got a private enquiry agency. I told Cameron that I needed his help. Don't worry about a thing. He'll do what he's told."

"Let's hope so for your sake," van Hall answered. "And remember, I don't want him anywhere near me, is that understood?"

"Understood," Hobart said. He hesitated, looking round the room curiously. "I was hoping we were going to have a chance to talk."

"Talk about what?" said van Hall, closing the curtains again.

Hobart's voice was hesitant. "Well, you know, the business. I might have ideas."

Van Hall looked at him appraisingly. "You're doing well, Henry, but the last thing I need at the moment is your ideas. Let me have the worries. All will be revealed in due course. I'll call you at home the day after tomorrow, 10 A.M. In the meantime don't let Cameron out of your sight. Hire a car and make sure he knows how to handle it."

FOUR

Rain had been falling since early morning, bringing with it the misery of November in London. The streets sprouted umbrellas. The traffic snarled up. Tempers grew shorter. It was seven o'clock in the evening.

Raven paid off the cab on Chelsea Embankment. The Ford Fiesta was parked in the cul-de-sac across the street, which meant that Kirstie was back from the studio. Raven had made a point of staying away from the boat all day, offering research for his book as a reason. It was low tide and the *Albatross* rose on mud at the foot of the steps. There were eighteen boats in the moorings, a motley collection of floating homes, custom-built houseboats, converted barges and a couple of upriver pleasure craft. Gangways led from an empty hull, connecting the boats to the shore. Raven and his neighbor shared their own private steps. The moorings provided power and telephone lines. The plumbing was Elsan, the water supplied by the Chelsea Yacht and Boat Company.

Raven had bought the *Albatross* fourteen years before, a newly promoted detective-inspector in the Metropolitan Police Force. At the time he was attached to New Scotland Yard and living in quarters. His move to Chelsea attracted the displeasure of his superiors. Possession of private means went against the tradition of the Force. Eccentric use of it made matters worse. The barge had once been used to haul grain. A hot summer's day still brought out the heady aroma of beer. He had spent thirty thousand pounds on the conversion. The interior of the hull had been planked over, a red cedarwood superstructure added. The blunt end of the barge comprised two large size bedrooms with a connecting bathroom. There was a kitchen, plenty of closet space and an enormous room that took up the rest of the boat's surface. Double-glazed panoramic windows offered views of the river, the shore and Battersea Park. An electric motor ran tangerine-colored velvet curtains to and fro on the rails. It was never completely dark on the boat. High tide, low tide, the river seemed to have its own incandescence.

The door at the bottom of the steps was festooned with razor-wire. There were two short gangways beyond the door. One led to Hank Lauterbach's rusting pinnace, the other to Raven's boat. The name *Albatross* was painted in flourishing script on the hull. There were no rails. Stanchions and a nylon rope ensured foothold. Raven walked along the deck. The curtains were drawn in the living-room windows. The barge was home to Raven in a way that the Paris apartment could never be. He'd courted Kirstie here, survived two attempts on his life here, composed the letter of resignation that had taken him out of the police-force. He opened the living-room door.

The long room was furnished haphazardly. The two matching couches bright with chintz covers had come from Kirstie's home in Toronto, as well as the silver. The much-darned Aubusson carpet and Jacobean writing bureau had come from Raven's maiden aunt. The Paul Klee hanging on the end wall was Raven's prized possession, a study in black and blue. He never tired of looking at it. A row of white-painted shelves and closets featured his tapes and records, the Bang and Olufsen Beocenter. Kirstie's Burberry and beret were on the back of a chair. The radio was playing in their bedroom. He went into the kitchen. The walls were painted apple-green. The Welsh dresser they had found in a Putney antique shop. Refrigerator, stove and freezing unit came from Zanussi. Small fish in the river below browsed on the groundup kitchen waste. He found an unfamiliar six-pack of beer in the refrigerator. The label read LABATT ASK FOR THE

BLUE   BOTTLED IN CANADA. Raven knocked the cap off a bottle and carried it through to his bedroom. Pink-shaded lamps made the room cosy and feminine. Kirstie was sitting on the end of the cane-headed bed, her legs drawn up, her shoes on the floor beside her. A shirt lay in her lap. She bent down and nipped the thread with her teeth.

"A button," she explained, pushing a lock of hair from her eyes.

"I can see that," he said. The shirt was not his. Furthermore, during the nine years they had lived together, he had never known his wife to sew on a button, not even one of her own.

She swung her stockinged feet from the bed, reached up and kissed him. He held her close, looking over her shoulder, through the open bathroom doors—into the guest room. His word-processor was still on the table, the sheet of paper with his pilot-outline in place on the wall. Kirstie walked through and placed the shirt on Cameron's bed. She came back, ruffling Raven's hair as she passed.

"And how was your day, my darling?"

"I've had better," he said, putting the empty beer bottle on the dressing table. "Where's Cameron?"

She was standing in front of the long cheval-mirror, mouth open, fiddling with an eye-lash.

"He went out," she said. Calvin Klein jeans made the most of her long legs and trim bottom. "He wanted to get the feel of the city, he said."

Wind drove the rain against the bedroom windows. "Odd time to do it," he said. He had seen no sign of supper in the kitchen. "When's he going to be back?"

"I have no idea," she said, turning round to face him. "There's a card from the Soos," she said, nodding towards the bureau.

He picked it up, smiling. The colored postcard portrayed Hindu erotic statuary. The script was in the Hong Kong–born cop's fancy style.

India! Womb of the World! My emotions and feelings would fill a book. The place stinks of shit. My third eye is slowly opening. Pray for me! Jerry

Detective-Inspector Soo's wife was a cellist. The quintet she played with had given a series of recitals in Bombay, Calcutta and

Delhi. Soo had taken leave from New Scotland Yard and accompanied her. The couple had been back in England for two days.

Raven followed Kirstie into the long sitting-room. She lit a few candles and put a record on the player. Raven slumped on a couch and closed his eyes. He opened them after a couple of minutes.

"Do we have to listen to that again?"

"Why not?" she demanded. "I like it."

Cameron had brought the record from Paris together with the longstemmed Cardinal roses in the vase and a carton of untipped Gitanes for Raven.

"I'm getting hungry," said Raven, changing the subject.

She lowered the volume a touch. For some reason his statement seemed to have brought her alive.

"I'll tell you what you're getting," she said. "You're getting to be a middle-aged mope. You've been back on the boat twenty minutes and you haven't stopped complaining."

"Is there something wrong about wanting to eat?" he demanded.

Kirstie made no reply.

"How long is Kirk going to be staying?" he said casually.

The look on her face would have blistered paint. "You really are something else," she said with her hands on her hips.

His shoulders rose and fell. "Just showing a natural interest."

"Does it bother you how long he's going to be here?" she said.

The fuse had been lit. There was no way of avoiding the explosion that would follow. Kirstie was fierce in defense of her friends.

"People come to stay," he said, "you usually have some idea how long it's going to be for."

She padded across to the drinks cupboard in her stockinged feet and poured herself a fierce campari-and-soda. She sat down opposite Raven, swirling the ice in her glass. Then she looked up.

"What exactly is it that you have against Kirk? You don't even *know* the man! He's been a very good friend to me."

"I've got nothing against him personally," Raven hedged. "I guess it's just that people who call themselves artists always make me nervous."

"Kirk doesn't call himself an artist," she said. "He's a painter and in my view a good one. Added to which, the only thing that makes you nervous is my driving. You're what my father used to call a cantankerous man."

"Do we have to go into this?" he pleaded. "I mean quoting your father's really below the belt."

"You started it," she said. "Let me ask you a question. Have I ever been unpleasant to any of your friends? Have I ever gone out of my way to make them feel unwelcome?"

Raven changed the record and re-started the player, his back to her. "I've never had an ex–girl-friend to stay."

She pounced like a cat on a mouse. "That, John, is pure effrontery! Kirk *isn't* an ex–boyfriend, not of mine, at least. He just happens to be part of my life, the same way as you are."

"Oh really?" he said, cocking an eyebrow. Kirstie would have been sixteen to Cameron's eighteen when they had been at school together. For some reason, he found himself remembering his own first sexual experience.

He grabbed her wrists, forcing her to meet his look. "I love you," he said, "and I don't like what's happening to us. We never used to fight like this. Tell me what's wrong."

She freed herself and kneaded the skin on her wrists, staring at him.

"The only thing that's gone wrong is inside your head. You invent these horrible monsters then you're scared of them. I ought to tell you, your friends are beginning to worry about you."

"Aha," he said, "here we go again. What friends are these and what are they worried about?"

The anger went from her face and her voice was suddenly gentle.

"Jerry Soo for one. I had coffee with Louise yesterday. Jerry told her that you barely spoke a word all the time you were up in Scotland together."

"Did he now?" he mocked, putting his head on one side. "Well, for your information, if you're standing up to your belly button in water that's as cold as a frog's tit with a six-pound salmon on the end of your line, you do not, repeat *not* feel like chitchat. And at the end of the day, you scratch your midge-bites and think about the fish that you lost. Added to which I don't give a fiddler's any longer who does what to who at the Yard."

"Jerry's not the only one," Kirstie said. "Patrick's worried too."

His laugh cracked. "That does it!" he said. "So my lawyer's in on the act. I find that strange, very odd. Whenever I see him, he says that I talk too much."

"You're intolerant," she said. "Even with people who love you. I mean, what happened in Paris this last time? You started the moment we got there. Everything was wrong. The cab drivers were licensed bandits; the apartment was uncomfortable; the PTT stank. Even your girl friend in the corner café got dishonorable mention, the glasses were dirty, you said. I don't know why you trouble to go there."

"I go there," he said in measured speech, "I go there to be with you, Kirstie."

"Not true," she said sadly. "You want to be where I *am*. You don't want to be with me."

The door slammed at the end of the gangway before he could take her in his arms. The Young Lochinvar had returned. Kirstie must have given him a key.

"Let's drop it," Raven said quickly.

They were both smiling welcome when Cameron stood in the doorway, shaking the rain from his clothes before he came into the room. Kirstie took his nylon mac.

"You're soaked," she said anxiously. She hung the mac in the kitchen and came back smiling. "I'll get you a beer," she said. "I got some Labatt!"

"She sewed a button on your shirt as well," said Raven, unable to resist it.

"You can bet it won't last," Cameron said, winking. "Does anyone happen to know where Onslow Gardens are?"

"What number?" said Raven. "They run all over the place."

"Thirty-eight," Cameron said. "It's someone I see when he comes to Paris."

"Thirty-eight?" Raven thought for a moment. "That's the continuation of Queen's Gate, South Kensington. You'll find it easily enough. You've got your key and you're free to come and go as you please. How long do you think you'll be staying?"

Kirstie's glare told him that he had drawn her fire again but he refused to back off.

Cameron shrugged rangy shoulders and put his beer on the table. Kirstie sat down beside him.

"A week or ten days," Cameron said. "There are people I have to see."

Kirstie showed interest. "Is there any chance of getting an exhibition over here?"

"It's a possibility," Cameron said, smiling.

A perverse will to lose drove Raven on. "So we might have you as a neighbor?"

Cameron tilted his head back and finished the last of his beer. "No chance. I'm too fond of Paris."

Kirstie looked at the clock. "It's twenty past eight. Do you still eat curry, Kirk?"

"Try me," he said. "The hotter the better. Remember that place on Spadina? They used to give you damp towels to wrap your head in. Man, that was hot!"

She unfurled her legs with one swift movement. "John'll book a table. Just give me five minutes to put on a face."

Raven followed her into the bedroom. He closed the doors to the bathroom and corridor. She slipped a black silk dress over her shoulders and narrow hips and considered herself in the mirror.

"You realize you're making a fool of yourself?" she said.

It was true, of course, but that only made matters worse. "I think the guy's bad news," he said quietly.

She rolled her lips and removed the excess rouge with a tissue.

"Well, he's here for a week at least and you'd better make him feel welcome. You don't have to like him. Just go through the motions."

He took a deep breath and returned to the sitting room. Cameron looked up from the newspaper.

"You can't win 'em all."

The expression of male solidarity came from the wrong quarter. Raven dialed the number of the Kubla Khan Restaurant.

FIVE

Hobart parked the Volkswagen twenty-five yards from Campion Court. Van Hall's Jaguar had been left nearby. He opened the door to the flat. Grey London light made van Hall's tan appear deeper. Hobart removed his raincoat.

"Sit down!" said van Hall, waving a hand.

The cane chair creaked under Hobart's weight. The air was as dead as the flies trapped in the double-glazing.

"I'm parched," Hobart said. "Is there anything to drink in the place?"

"I'll make you some coffee," van Hall replied. He moved casually, sure of himself. Water ran in the kitchen. He was back in a couple of minutes, a mug in his hand. He put it down in front of Hobart. "So tell me about Cameron."

Hobart tasted the coffee. It came from a jar. "He's Okay. We rented a car from Hertz. He had to give his right name because of his driving license. He gave the address of these people in Chelsea. He's a good driver. I've been showing him round the back doubles. He soon got the hang of the traffic."

Van Hall leaned against the mantel. The two-bar heater in the firegrate burned faintly.

"I rented a box in the Hans Security Vaults."

Hobart picked at the skin on a knuckle. He stayed silent.

"You don't have a lot to say for yourself," said van Hall.

Hobart shifted uneasily. "You told me in Paris. You ask too many questions, you said."

"This is different," van Hall told him. "Why do you think I rented this box?"

Hobart shrugged and looked away through the window. Men dressed in yellow slickers were emptying garbage cans into the maw of a truck.

"I've no idea," he confessed. "Something to do with Sheffield? That's about as far as my imagination takes me."

"Right," said van Hall. "You're going to break into his locker. We have reached Phase Two of the operation."

He took an expensively printed pamphlet from his briefcase and laid it open on the table.

"There it is, Hans Security Vaults, open for our inspection. Read! The building is made of steel-reinforced concrete. Only the two lower floors concern us. The offices on the upper floors are reached through the Sloane Street entrance. Is there something the matter with your coffee, Henry?"

Hobart shook his head, nervous under the other man's scrutiny. He sipped from the mug again. "I was listening to what you were saying."

Van Hall leaned forward under the hundred-watt lamp in the ceiling. His scalp was sunburned at the back where his hair thinned. He pointed down at a colored photograph showing a uniformed guard standing in front of a row of safety-deposit boxes. He read from the text. " 'Each customer receives a factory-sealed capsule containing his personal lock. The lock is installed in the customer's presence. There is only one key. Its loss requires the services of the makers to open the locker. A deposit of two hundred and fifty pounds is required against such eventuality.' That's to encourage you to be careful," said van Hall. "The name of the makers is Paragon Locks. There's only one place in London where you can buy their products."

He pulled a brown paper bag from a drawer in the table. It contained a metal cylinder.

"They only sell the genuine article to Hans Security," said van Hall, handing the cylinder to Hobart. "But this is the same type. Take a good look at it."

Hobart took the small barrel in his hands. It was made of high-grade steel, an inch long, a half-inch in diameter. There were two retractible studs, one on each side of the barrel. Hobart turned the key in the lock. The studs emerged smoothly. In this position, they would hold a lock in its housing.

Van Hall took a similar key from his pocket. The flat end of the shank bore a number.

"This is the key to my box, Henry. Sheffield's is in the row below. The problem is getting into his locker. How are you going to do it?"

Hobart bent his head, his fingers covering his mouth. He looked up. "Is there anyone else in there with you? I mean when you're taking something out of your locker?"

Van Hall shook his head. "The security guard stays outside the room. There are some cubicles where you can use the phone or the Xerox machine."

Hobart thought for a moment. "Suppose another customer's in there with you?"

"There won't be," van Hall said with assurance. "That much I can guarantee."

Hobart returned the lock to its wrapping. "This is high-tech engineering. I couldn't get near it with the kind of equipment I've got. You could sit for a week in front of something like this, diddling around and getting nowhere. On the other hand, I know someone who could solve the problem, but he'd be expensive."

Van Hall frowned. "We can't afford to have anyone else in, Henry. There's too much at stake."

"It's the last thing this guy would want," replied Hobart. "He just makes tools. He does what he has to do, gets paid and that's that. He doesn't care what you do with the article. Any questions, he never saw it. He's the only person I can think of who'd be able to help. But like I say, he's expensive."

Van Hall replaced the cylinder in his briefcase. "And you think he can do it?"

"I *know* he can, the man's an artist."

"How much would this cost, four, five hundred? More?"

"I don't know. He'd have to see the lock. I'll tell him that I need something in a hurry. He doesn't work regular hours."

"Nor do we." Van Hall's smile was bleak. He opened his brief-case again as though on an afterthought. He extracted the lock-barrel and a small sheaf of fifty-pound notes. "Just keep track of what you spend," he said. "You haven't asked me how you'll get into the vault, Henry."

Hobart put the fifty-pound notes in his pocket. He was feeling more sure of himself.

"Ok, how will I get into the vault?"

Van Hall passed what looked like a credit card across the table. It was made of plastic and bore the same number as the key to van Hall's locker. The name "Alan Bailey" was written in ink in the space provided.

"That's me, Alan Bailey," said van Hall. "Nobody gives his right name in those places. This card gets you into the customers' car park, underneath Hans Security. Do you know Pavilion Road?"

Hobart bobbed his head. "It runs up from King's Road, parallel with Sloane Street."

"Correct," said van Hall. "The front entrance to the Vaults is in Sloane Street, but the car park's behind in Pavilion Road. I want you to take a good look at the place before Sunday."

A nerve crawled on Hobart's neck. "What happens on Sunday?"

Van Hall's smile was bland. "That's when you go in, Henry. The Vaults are open from two until seven on Sundays. There are only two guards on duty. They're Asians and they're not paid to be heroes."

He stopped suddenly. "For crissakes, sit down, Henry. You're making me nervous." He waited until Hobart settled himself in his chair again. Then he continued. "The card gets you into the lift in the car park as well. There's only one stop up to the Vaults. You come out of the lift and turn left. You'll see a steel door with an optic. The guard inside takes a look at you and you show him the card. That's the first check that you're a bona-fide customer. He lets you in through the door. Now it gets difficult. He'll ask you to put your right hand on the scanner. Your prints are supposed to match the ones that they've got on file. Yours won't, of course, so you show him the gun."

"The gun." Hobart felt his voice slipping away and retrieved it. "What gun?"

Van Hall leaned back, crossing his legs and looking at Hobart. "I want you to listen to me, Henry," he said in a low earnest tone.

"I know what you think. You see the Jaguar, the clothes, the glitzy lifestyle and you think I'm an asshole. I can understand that. But there's another side to it, Henry. I'm in big trouble with the bank. I went to South America on a deal that would have got me out of trouble. Sheffield took that deal away from me. What he's got in the safety-deposit box belongs to me. Do you understand? It's my property."

Hobart cleared the lump in his throat. "Nobody mentioned a gun."

"That's right," said van Hall. "If I'd told you the truth in Paris, you'd still be running. Not only that, there were things that I had to do first. This isn't going to one of those half-cock scams with Inspector Knacker charging around looking for clues. This is going to be foolproof, Henry, performed by people without criminal records. A few minutes' work and the whole thing will be over. We all go our respective ways. You know that my promise is good. Do this with me and you'll be rich by Sunday night. Cash on delivery."

Hobart blinked. Van Hall's manner was almost hypnotic. "I thought you said you were broke."

"I am," said van Hall. "But the bank can't afford to throw me overboard, not for this kind of money. Look, if it makes you any happier, the gun doesn't have to be loaded."

Hobart's laugh came out as a croak. "If I get busted with a gun, it doesn't mean a shit if it's loaded or not. I'll be inside the nick for a very long time. What's the good of two hundred grand if you're banged up, stitching mailbags?"

Van Hall's manner held conviction. "You won't *be* caught, Henry, I give you my word on it. Look, I'm up to my neck in this. I'm taking every precaution possible. You'll see. There'll be nobody in the place on Sunday except you, Cameron and the two Pakistanis. Think about it. Someone sticks a gun in your face, what do you do?"

"I do whatever he tells me to do," Hobart said promptly.

"Precisely," said van Hall. He pulled a Spanish-made thirty-two caliber automatic from his pocket and gave it to Hobart. "The clip's full. Make sure you keep the safety-catch on. That way you won't blow your dick off."

Hobart dropped the gun in his raincoat pocket. What had started as a lighthearted trip down Larceny Lane had turned into

Assault with a Deadly Weapon. But so what. Costa Rica was waiting. He reached for a cigarette. He had kicked the habit twice in
six months and here he was back on it. His lighter flared and he
spoke between puffs.

"There's no way that Cameron's going to hold still for any of
this, no way at all."

"I didn't expect him to," van Hall replied. "You've got to give
him a story that'll cover the facts as he'll see them. He doesn't
have to know about the gun, Henry. He drives you down to the
car park. You go up in the lift alone. After fifteen, twenty minutes, you're down with the goodies. He doesn't see guards, he
doesn't see people. All he sees is this big grin on your face. What
have you told him so far?"

Hobart's mind jumped like a hare with a hound on its tail. "He
thinks he's helping me out on this case. I'm supposed to be working for this lawyer on the custody thing. Don't worry about Cameron, everything's under control. What am I supposed to be looking for?"

"Just a few papers, Henry. They're of no value to anyone except me. Sheffield couldn't get a penny for them."

"But you can," said Hobart. He was still grappling with the
promise of two hundred thousand pounds cash. It was hard to
believe, yet van Hall inspired confidence.

Van Hall leaned forward. "Politics, Henry," he said, laying a
forefinger alongside his nose. "These papers belong to me. As
long as they're in Sheffield's possession, he's got his hands round
my throat. He won't let go until he's throttled me."

"If they're there, you'll have them," Hobart promised. All this
was a long way from standing in someone's back yard, rain pour-
ing down the nape of your neck, watching a set of drawn curtains. This was big league.

Van Hall glanced up from inspecting his nails. "We still haven't
solved the problem of getting into the box. The gun'll only get
you into the vaults from the car park."

"Can I use the phone?" Hobart asked.

Van Hall waved a hand. "Help yourself."

A man's voice answered the call. "Devonport Engineering."

"It's Henry Hobart, Steve. I'd like you to do me a favor."

"I don't do no more favors," the voice said sourly. "Last time I
done someone a favor, the geezer took off with my wife."

"I need to see you tonight," Hobart said. "A little job you can do for me. It's urgent. The money's up front."

"I close at six," said the voice. "Drop round after that. Ring the doorbell."

Hobart replaced the phone. "I'd better be on my way. I've got to see Cameron later on."

Van Hall passed a couple of keys across. "Be here same time tomorrow. You can let yourself in. If I'm not here, wait."

Van Hall came as far as the door to the hallway. The gun and the lock-barrel sagged in Hobart's pockets, one on each side. The two men shook hands. Van Hall's face broke into a slow smile.

"I'm going to miss you, Henry. You're the right stuff."

Hobart's next stop was in a shabby neighborhood near Shepherd's Bush Green. He parked in front of the usual Indian corner store. A row of boarded-up houses stretched to a defunct chapel. The board on the yard out front read DEVONPORT ENGINEERING. Lights burned behind dirty windows. Hobart rang the doorbell. Bolts were retracted. The door scraped open. The man standing inside was in his sixties with a bald head, pearshaped nose and suspicious eyes. He wore oilstained overalls and smelled of carbolic. His gaze fixed on the package in Hobart's hand.

"I see you, what, twice a year," he said ungraciously. "And you talk about favors. You never done a favor in your bleeding life."

Hobart grinned. "How've you been, Steve? Long time no see."

"I've been a whole lot better," said Steve King. He took a quick glance up and down the street and rebolted the door. "What do you want?" he demanded.

The machine shop was the size of a tennis court with belt-driven lathes and hand-presses. Oil drums were filled with tin-plate offcuts. An amalgam of dirt and grease filled every crevice, and the concrete floor was heavily stained. The odor attached to King came from the carbolized liquid used to cool highspeed machinery.

Hobart moved his feet with the care of a cat confronted with water.

"Can we talk sitting down?" he asked.

King wiped his hands on his filthy overalls. His bare forearms were tattooed. A slide rule stuck out of a pocket. He led the way through confusion to a plasterboard office erected at the back of

the shop. The one uncurtained window offered a view of the
Underground embankment. There was a table with a phone on it,
a couple of metal files, two chairs and a gas-ring with a kettle.
Steve King took the chair behind the table.

"What's your problem?" he said, leaning back in his chair.

Hobart unwrapped the lock-barrel and placed it on the table
between them. Steve King commanded respect among the people
who used him. Few knew where he lived. He was a secret man
whose sole interest apart from his work was reading military history.

"You know these things, of course," Hobart asked, nodding
down at the lock-barrel.

King turned it over a couple of times with spatulate fingers. "I
know 'em," he said shortly.

"It's for a friend of mine," Hobart elaborated. "He's a player.
There's this woman got a safe in her bedroom. My friend wants
to get into it. The safe's got one of these locks on it."

The older man pushed the cylinder back towards Hobart. "No
chance," he said. "Not with a twirl, at any rate."

"That's what I told him," Hobart said. "He's ready to pay good
money for the right piece of gear. That's why I thought of you."

"Don't give me that shit," said Steve King. "You're out to earn
like everyone else."

He took the lock in his hands again and used a powerful magni-
fying glass on it.

"Beautiful piece of engineering," he said, shaking his head.
"How much time has your friend got?"

"Not too long," Hobart said.

"You'll have to do better than that," said the older man. "Okay,
he's in the room where the safe is. How long has he got before
somebody blows the whistle?"

"Fifteen minutes, twenty. Twenty's the limit."

"Can he get at the power-points?"

"I'm not sure," Hobart said. "I know there are lights."

"If you're not sure, forget it," said King. "What I had in mind
would blow your ordinary light circuits. A clamp's the only alternative."

His dark eyes roved the room. He placed the lock on its side on
the table.

"There's your lock in the safe," he said. "Everything's flush.

You're looking at a totally flat surface, run your finger over the face of it, no breaks. Right?"

Hobart nodded.

King mimed each move that followed. "The key's turned. Everything's fixed in position. The weakest point of the lock is these two studs. They'll snap under pressure but the only way to apply pressure is through the keyhole. So you got a problem."

Hobart jerked his head again.

King was in full flow by now. "You need something you can insert in the lock through the keyhole, something that's stronger than the lock itself." He brought the heels of his hands together, fingertips touching the face of the lock. "This here's a tripod with one end of your rod attached to it. The other end's got a ratchet and pawl so the wheel can't lose purchase." He cranked his right arm. "Now comes your pressure. The studs got to give. The whole lock-barrel comes out like one of your teeth. Better still, one of mine." He widened his grin, revealing National Health dentures.

Hobart was hesitant. "Do you think it'll work?"

"Put four hundred quid on the table and I'll guarantee it'll work," King replied.

"My friend's got to have it tonight."

King glanced at the clock on the wall. "There's all I need right here on the premises. A couple of hours should do it. You come back about nine, say, and I'll have it ready. I'll have a mock-up as well, show you how the thing works."

Hobart peeled off eight of the fifty-pound notes van Hall had given him.

"I'll see you at nine," he said.

SIX

The barge had lifted on the incoming tide and rocked with a gentle movement. It was Saturday morning, Kirstie's day off from the studio. She was reading a newspaper, wearing a Victorian nightdress with lace on the sleeves. Her elbows were propped on the kitchen table, her hair piled high on top of her head. Raven wore striped flannel pyjamas, and had the *Times* crossword in front of him. Cameron was the only one dressed for the street. The radio was playing on the kitchen dresser. No-one had spoken for the last twenty minutes. Relations between Raven and Cameron had cooled to a wary acceptance of each other's presence.

Cameron reached for his cigarettes. "Does anyone mind if I smoke?"

Kirstie moved her head from side to side without looking up. Raven said nothing. Cameron placed his breakfast things in the sink and took his cigarettes through to the sitting room. He was finding Raven increasingly difficult to deal with. Raven was civil enough, especially if Kirstie was present. At other times he remained aloof. The sitting room curtains were open. Smoke came from the stack of the neighboring boat. The American who lived there owned the Oriental gift-shop in the alleyway across the street. He had given Cameron permission to park his rented car there.

Cameron flopped on a couch and lifted the phone. He asked for a reverse-charge call to Irma Hoenigsberg's number in Paris. There was an hour's difference in time but she was still in her apartment. Her *r*'s rolled like a drumbeat and she spat her sibilants.

"Where are you?" she cried in English. "Are you crazy or what? What are you doing in London? Who is this woman?"

He held the noise away from his ear until she paused to draw breath.

"Don't be ridiculous," he said. "There is no woman. I'm spending a few days with friends in London, that's all."

Her voice was laced with suspicion. "These people, these friends, who are they?"

"They're not dealers," he said patiently. "Listen, I've had a stroke of luck. Someone's lending me the money to rent Eugène Decker's studio. I want you to get hold of him, tell him I'll be back in Paris on Monday. Tell him not to let the studio go to anyone else, I'll give him a year's rent in advance."

Mention of money always unsettled her. "I hope you're not asking me to act as your banker," she said tartly.

"I wouldn't be as daft as that," he said. "Just tell him what I said. I'll give him a year's rent, in advance, on Monday. Will you do that for me, Irma?"

She made a noise through her nose. "The only time I hear from you is when you want something. Does this mean that you're going to be working seriously?"

"It means that I'll have a place of my own again. Somewhere with decent light, a place of my own. Do you know how to get hold of Eugène?"

Her voice rattled in the diaphragm. "In the café, where else? With the rest of your other friends."

"Goodbye for now," he said quickly. "I'll see you on Monday." He put the phone down and went back to the kitchen. He poured himself another cup of coffee.

"My heart sinks at the thought of going back to all that." He sat down at the table again.

Kirstie put her newspaper down. "Then *why* go back?" she challenged. "Stay here. We'll find you somewhere to live."

"I mean going back to Irma, not Paris," he said.

She unbound her hair, letting it fall loose to her shoulders. "Monday! The time's gone so quickly. Listen, Kirk, why don't you let me ask around. I'm sure we can find you a studio."

Raven came to life, eyes still half-closed as though he had been dozing.

"The man knows what he's doing, Kirstie. Artists need the right surroundings. It's the way they are."

"The way they are," she repeated, looking at her husband scathingly. She flung a hand out at Cameron. "This is a man," she told him, nodding at Raven, "who takes pride in saying that he did the Prado in twenty-two minutes!"

Cameron laughed, viewing her fondly. Wearing no make-up she was the teenager he had been close to for nearly four years, his comrade and confidante. These last few days had reforged the bond between them. The thought that he hadn't been frank with Kirstie or Raven troubled him. It would have been better to tell them the truth. Kirstie at least would have understood if not approved.

"Tomorrow's Sunday," Cameron said, looking from one to the other. "My last day. I've got some people to see but I'll be through by the evening. I'd like to take you people out to supper."

"Good one," said Raven. "We'd like that, wouldn't we, Kirstie?" He patted her hand.

"Then that's settled," said Cameron, pulling his chair back and rising. "I'll leave it to you to choose the venue."

He pulled the raincoat over the green corduroy suit and went out on deck. He climbed the steps, walked across the Embankment and drove the rented Rover out of the cul-de-sac. His rendezvous with Hobart was in a multi-storey car park on the corner of Hans Place and Pavilion Road. He collected his ticket from the machine at the foot of the ramp and drove up to the top floor. Hobart's Volkswagen was the only other car there. Hobart climbed out, dragging the skirts of his long black raincoat. He was wearing a paneled cap and dark glasses. He motioned Cameron to join him at the parapet and pointed down at the street.

"Beyond the entrance to the Chelsea Hotel, can you see the estate agent?"

Cameron peered over the brickwork. "No," he said shortly.

"For crissakes," Hobart said, "you're not even looking in the right direction!" He grabbed Cameron's arm and swung him around. "Down there!" he urged.

"Got it," said Cameron.

"Ok. There's a big door in the wall painted grey next to it."

"I see it," said Cameron. "There's what looks like a cash-dispenser at the side."

Hobart stepped back from the parapet, his dark glasses mirroring Cameron. He pulled a plastic card from his pocket.

"Stick this in the wall," he said, holding the card in the air, "and the door goes up. It takes a couple of seconds before it starts working. There's a ramp down to the car park. An electronic eye stops you getting chopped halfway down. As soon as you're safely below, the door comes down again. You're looking at the Hans Security Vaults car park."

Hobart removed his cap and dark glasses. They sat together in the front of Cameron's rented car. Hobart's manner had changed since Cameron had arrived in London. He seemed much more sure of himself. His conversation was almost entirely about Julia Benson, his client, and her difficulties with her husband. Hobart had taken Cameron to the Dorchester Hotel and pointed out a man sitting alone at the bar.

"Francis Benson," Hobart had said. According to Hobart, Benson was a man in his late thirties, a stockbroker. Cameron learned that Mrs. Benson had gone to Saint Lucia with a man, leaving her five-year-old daughter in London with relatives. A private detective employed by Benson had followed her to the West Indies. He had broken into her villa and stolen some pictures and negatives. These formed the basis of the divorce action Benson was bringing against his wife. Benson sought custody of his daughter. Whoever had custody of the child controlled a two-million-pound trust fund.

It was quiet on the rainswept deck of the car park. "It's the first time I've ever had a job like this," Hobart said. "With money no object and the chance to use my head. I pull this one off, Kirk, I'm made for life."

"It means a lot to me, too," said Cameron. "It means a place to live and work without Irma Hoenigsberg shafting me."

"Mrs. Benson won't go back on her word," said Hobart. "She likes the scheme I've come up with. You get your money in cash tomorrow night. She's a grateful woman. And so she should be, what we're doing for her."

Cameron stretched out his legs and worried a cigarette out of the pack.

"You haven't told me yet exactly what we're doing for her."

"We're going into the Vaults tomorrow afternoon," Hobart said. "Benson's got a safety-deposit in there. That's where he keeps the photographs. According to Farrell, the lawyer, they ought to carry X certificates, for Adult Viewing Only. But that's none of our business. All we're doing is providing a service."

Cameron thought about it for a few seconds. "You know something," he said. "I never thought of myself as being dumb, but I don't understand. Benson's got hold of these photographs, right? Why would he give them to you?"

"He won't," Hobart said, smiling. His smile slid away. "I'm going to take them."

"Makes sense," Cameron said. He gestured at the building across the street. "You've got these pictures in a box over there. Alarms all over the place. Armed guards for all I know. And you're just going to *take* them! You're out of your head is what I think!"

Hobart laid a hand on Cameron's sleeve. "Do you trust me, Kirk?"

"I trust everyone," Cameron said, grinning. "Winos with three-carat diamonds to sell, cross-eyed bull mastiffs, and strangers who show me the way. I trust everything and everybody. I'm just looking for information, Henry. I need money at the moment but it sure isn't worth going to jail for."

"Nobody's going to jail. I know what I'm doing," Hobart argued. "A chance in a lifetime, this is. And you know something else, Kirk? There isn't another guy in London who could have put this together. That's why they came to me. We do it tomorrow afternoon. All you do is drive and that's it. The rest is down to me."

Cameron shifted his weight. "I stay below in the car and you go up to the Vaults. There are guards up there, right? Armed guards and Benson. What are you going to use, a bazooka?"

Hobart shrank inside his long black raincoat, his small eyes resentful.

"What are you, a comedian all of a sudden? Do I *look* like a gunman? There are only two guards on duty tomorrow and they're both on our side. They're going to be found trussed like chickens. They won't be able to remember any more than the lights went out. They won't even *see* you in any case. You think I want to go to jail? They've been *paid*, Kirk."

It was difficult to resist Hobart's assertions but Cameron still had misgivings.

"Ok. What happens if someone else walks in on the performance? Other people will be coming in and out of the place."

Hobart walked across to the Volkswagen. He came back carrying a cardboard cylinder. He shook out a printed notice. It read:

HANS SECURITY VAULTS
THE MANAGEMENT REGRETS THAT THESE PREMISES
ARE TEMPORARILY CLOSED FOR TECHNICAL REASONS.
NORMAL SERVICE WILL BE RESUMED TOMORROW.

"There are two of them," Hobart said. "The moment the guards are safely inside the building, we put up the notices. One on the Sloane Street entrance, the other round the back on Pavilion Road. The thing to remember is, these guards are earning enough to keep them and their families for the next couple of years." Saliva sprayed from his mouth. His look was excited.

"Get a hold on yourself," Cameron said, wiping his hand with his handkerchief. "Ok, it's against all I was taught as a boy. It's the lure of the money I can't resist."

Hobart fiddled with the peak of his cap. "You know you worry me?"

The smile faded from Cameron's face. "How's that?"

"It's your attitude," Hobart said. "This is serious business. A woman's reputation's at stake, a child's future. It's my one big chance, for crissakes, and you sit there with a big fat grin on your face."

Cameron took his time answering. "Well," he said finally, "I'll tell you. A week ago, you asked me to believe any of this bullshit I'd have run. There are too many unanswered questions. But I look at it this way. You say there's no chance of the police getting involved, I have to believe you. You're not the suicidal type and it's your ass on the line, not mine. I'm just the driver. So all that and the thought of money in my hot little hand keeps me cheerful."

Hobart eased himself out of the hired car and leaned back through the open doorway.

"Remember that hotel where we ate lunch a couple of days ago, the Grosvenor at Victoria?"

Cameron nodded.

"Meet me there one-thirty tomorrow afternoon. It'll be Sunday. You'll have no problem parking."

Cameron closed his right eye in a jovial hint of conspiracy. "Don't worry about a thing."

Hobart waited in the Volkswagen until the other car had cleared the ramp. He drove north to Brompton Road. American Express had his tickets ready. His next stop was the Diocesan Travel Agency behind Westminster Cathedral. There was a picture of the Pope on the wall of the office, a gilt-and-plaster statuette of Saint Teresa. The girl behind the desk scribbled a receipt for Hobart's money and gave him a travel folder.

"Have a joyful time in Portugal," she said. "I made the pilgrimage with my mother last year and it really does work. She had this hipbone disease. Inoperable, so the doctors said. She's back walking like a twenty-year-old."

Hobart bought a blue-and-white seersucker suit and Madras cotton shirts in the Army and Navy store. Back in the car, he removed the labels from the clothes with a pair of nail scissors. It was ten past nine when he finally parked close to the Brompton Chest Hospital. He checked the empty glove compartment and the baggage space in the front end of the car, ensuring that nothing had been left that would denote ownership. He wrapped the ignition keys in a fifty-pound note, put both items in an envelope that he pushed inside the tail-pipe. He walked to the nearest payphone and dialed. The coin dropped and a voice replied.

"Corner of Neville Street and Fulham Road," Hobart said. "The keys and the money are inside the exhaust pipe."

"I'm on my way," said the voice.

Hobart stepped out of the booth. By Monday, the Volkswagen would be reduced to yet another block of metal in a carbreaker's yard. There would be no claim for insurance. The car would just disappear. He turned up his collar and pulled his cap down. It was raining again. The traffic was heavy on Onslow Gardens. Hobart gained access to the house by way of the basement steps. The only article left in the safe was the thirty-two automatic. He slipped the gun into his pocket, leaving the safe open, the key in the lock, the way it had been when he first found it. The rest of its contents had been dumped. He retraced his steps to the street, dropped the basement key down a storm-grating and entered the house through the front door. He stood in the hallway, listening. The pattern of sound was normal for Saturday night. Most of the younger tenants were out, the older ones in their flats, eating takeaway Tandoori and watching television. It was the way in which he had lived for the past three years. He reminded himself that this would be the last time he climbed the sixty-eight stairs to his flat. When he left tomorrow, it would be forever.

He opened his door. The drawers and cupboards had been emptied, the contents dumped at a Salvation Army pickup point. There was nothing left in the flat that belonged to him except the things on the bed, the flight bag and canvas holdall containing the extractor that Steve King had made, the two printed notices and a roll of heavy-duty adhesive tape. He put the gun under his pillow and removed the girl's photograph from the frame on the bedside table. He tore the picture in four and pulled the lavatory chain on the pieces. So much for that piece of self-indulgence. He sat on the bed and unlocked the flight-bag. The Republic of Ireland passport inside bore Hobart's picture and the name "Francis Wilson," born April 17, 1956, in Ashford, County Wicklow. The bearer was described as a schoolteacher.

Hobart took the two tickets from his pocket. The one issued by the American Express was for an Iberia flight from Lisbon to San José, Costa Rica, by way of Madrid and Caracas. The name of the passenger was Francis Wilson. The flight was timed to leave Lisbon at 17.00 Hrs on Monday. There was a five-hour wait at Barajas Airport. From Madrid he flew to San José. He was due to arrive in Costa Rica later on Wednesday night. He slipped the Irish passport inside the American Express folder and buried it under the seersucker suit. The second travel folder contained the charter-flight ticket from Gatwick to Oporto and back. The flight left Gatwick early on Monday morning and returned three days later. A printed form was attached to the flight coupon.

DEVOTEES OF SAINT TERESA WELCOME
TO THE LAND OF MIRACLES
Your flight will be met by Father Aníbal Mesquita SJ. An air-

conditioned bus will transport you to the Hotel Lusitania. All
rooms are equipped with central-heating and colour tv.

MONDAY   Visit to the cathedral.

TUESDAY   10 am Pilgrims will be bussed to the Shrine of Our
Lady of Fatima where they may make their devotions. Bus
returns to Oporto at six pm. The same routine will be followed
during the rest of your stay. Your return flight leaves Oporto
airport at twenty hours local time on Thursday. Pilgrims will be
under the aegis of Father Mesquita at all times.

Hobart put the charter-flight ticket and his British passport in
his overnight bag. Henry Hobart would leave the airplane in
Oporto complaining of chest pains. He'd volunteer a history of
angina to the priest in charge of the party and state his intention
of returning to England forthwith. He'd make his own way
home. At five o'clock on Monday afternoon Francis Wilson
would leave Lisbon enroute for Costa Rica.

Hobart drew back the curtains, turned out the lights and
stretched out on the bed. Lying with his head on the pillows, he
could see the wet slate roofs and the floodlit dome of the Victoria
and Albert Museum. Reality had always destroyed his glimpses of
fantasy. Now all that was about to change. Just a few more hours
and he would leave Onslow Gardens forever. The rent of his flat
was paid until June. The woman who cleaned had no key, no
reason to query his absence. He would be numbered among the
two thousand people who disappeared every day of the year in
the city. A vision of San José was clear in his mind, a city of
flowers and colonial mansions. There'd be a few high rise buildings to keep up with progress. By and large it would be a good
place to live in. The money he was getting from van Hall was
never far from his thoughts, a magical sum that would erase all
difficulties. He'd buy a modest apartment, learn Spanish and look
around for something to do. In this goddam country he earned no
respect. It would be different in Costa Rica.

It was a quarter to eight when he waked. Sunday morning with
the rain coming down and the church bells pealing. He bathed
and donned his blazer and slacks. He took one last look round the
flat, wondering who would next open it. There was no sound
outside on the landing. His neighbors slept long on the day of
rest. He made his way down to the street, tossed his house keys in

a builder's skip and waited in the lee of an Old Brompton Road
doorway until a cab pulled up at his signal. He drove to the Grosvenor Hotel, where he exchanged pounds for dollars. He deposited the dollars in the overnight bag with his passports, flight
tickets and clothing. He locked the bag and left it with the hall
porter. He would retrieve it later, he said. Hobart bought a couple of newspapers and carried the overnight bag with Steve
King's clamp and the two notices into the restaurant. He spent an
hour over breakfast, the automatic in the inside left pocket of his
blazer. Breakfast finished, he found a seat in the lobby. People
were checking out at the desk, carrying baggage through to the
station. Cameron arrived five minutes early. He stood near the
entrance, scanning the lobby and staircase. Locating Hobart, the
Canadian raised a finger and walked across.

"How you doing?" he said, winking.

Hobart found the insouciant attitude irksome. But he made
nothing of it, remembering that as far as the Canadian was concerned the whole thing was some sort of caper.

"Where are you parked?" Hobart asked.

Cameron nodded towards the bus station.

"Let's get out of here," Hobart said and picked up the blue
canvas bag. They hurried through the rain to the rented Rover.
The two men sat in the front seats.

"We'll go over this, one last time," Hobart said. "We don't want
any cockups. We wait until we see the two guards arrive, right?
Then we go round to Pavilion Road. I open up with the card and
we drive down the ramp. No problems, right?"

"Right," agreed Cameron. He gave one of his patented grins.

Hobart narrowed his eyes even more. "This isn't a bleeding
joke, you know. This is serious business. You turn the car round
just as soon as I head for the lift. You wait until you hear the lift
coming down again, then you start the motor. You don't get out
of the car, understand? You do *not* get out of the car."

"Cool," said Cameron, trailing his fingers across the scar on his
cheekbone as if establishing its contours. "About the money," he
said. "When are we getting paid?"

Hobart rolled his eyes at the roof. "The money again! I thought
we'd got that straightened out."

"I heard what you told me," the Canadian said. "It just didn't answer my questions. I'd like to know when and where. I have things to do."

"We all do," said Hobart. "Just as soon as we're through at the Vaults, you'll drive me to Regent's Park. That's where we're paid."

"Is that the woman's place or the lawyer's?" queried Cameron.

Hobart ignored the question. "The money was drawn from the bank on Friday. I've already seen it," lied Hobart. "You'll be back in Paris before midnight."

"Not me," said Cameron. "I'm staying over until tomorrow." His eyes grew curious. "You never did tell me how much you're making out of this business."

"More than you are," said Hobart, grunting as he buckled his seatbelt. "But that's as it should be. I'm doing most of the work. Ok, let's move it."

They had already rehearsed the run from Victoria to Sloane Street. Cameron drove with attention, checking the rearview mirror from time to time.

"No time for conversations with the constabulary," he said, winking again.

They came to a halt fifty yards away from the main entrance to the Hans Security Vaults. Sloane Street was practically deserted. A few tourists clustered in front of Kurt Geiger and Vuitton, window-shopping. Hobart kept looking at his watch. Two Pakistanis turned the corner, emerging from Knightsbridge Underground station.

"That's them," Hobart said, slipping out of his seatbelt. "Keep your head down."

Cameron sneaked a quick glance before bending low. The older guard appeared to be in his forties, dark-skinned and wearing a uniform under his raincoat. His partner was younger and wearing the same type of uniform. He was the one who carried the umbrella. The two men climbed the three steps leading to the Vaults entrance. Beyond the plateglass windows was a lobby paved with marble. The older man produced a bunch of keys and unlocked the glass entrance doors. He touched a switch on the wall and crossed the lobby with his colleague.

Hobart waited until they had disappeared before grabbing one of the rolled-up notices.

"Drive round the back," he ordered. "Get the car in position and wait for me there. And remember, don't pay attention to nobody."

He opened the passenger door. Cameron had the car moving as Hobart climbed the three steps. The glass door was open, the lobby empty. A bronze and steel portico led to the Vaults. Hobart fixed the printed message to the inside of the glass entrance door and slipped the catch so that the door closed shut behind him. He hurried round the corner onto Pavilion Road. A porter was loading baggage into a cab in the rain. No-one paid attention as Hobart fixed the second notice on the massive steel door. Cameron had the Rover facing the wall. Hobart fed the plastic card into the slot. Signals on the magnetic strip triggered the correct electric impulses. The steel door began to rise. The words PLEASE REMOVE YOUR CARD appeared in a window above the slot. Hobart retrieved it and followed the car down the ramp. The Rover broke the circuit at the bottom, sending the door back on its upward journey. It was closed by the time Cameron had swung the Rover in a u-turn to face the ramp. The Canadian lowered his window and made a circle with thumb and forefinger. There was room below for twenty cars. Stenciled signs on the oil-stained concrete allotted the parking spaces.

The ceiling was twenty feet high, the weight supported by painted steel girders. A low hum came from the room on the left. Straight ahead was the lift-shaft. On the right of this was the emergency staircase. Hobart pulled down the peak of his cap, picked up the bag and walked across to the lift. He used the plastic card for the second time. The lift doors opened immediately. He stepped forward into the car. The interior was padded in burgundy leather. A telephone was fixed to the wall in case of emergency. An oblong mirror reflected the upper half of Hobart's body. The tilted cap gave him a note of menace. He emerged into a short corridor with a steel door at the end. A surveillance camera high on the wall tracked Hobart's passage as far as the door. An eye inspected him through the optic. The guard spoke into the voice-box.

"PIN number, please."

Hobart read the digits from the plastic card. Machinery whirred and the door opened. The younger of the two guards faced Hobart across a metal table. The initials HSV were embroidered in gilt thread on the lapels of his tunic. His cap was cocked

at a General MacArthur angle. He considered Hobart incuri-
ously, behaving as he did a hundred times during the week.

"Good afternoon, sir," he said, offering a token smile.

They were in an anteroom with a short passage running off to
the right. Hobart could see the rows of lockers through a grille
beyond the guard. An apparatus for confirming a customer's fin-
gerprints was lodged on top of the table between them. The result came up on a small screen. The guard spoke with a plummy
accent, his right foot close to the panic-button set in the floor.

"It is necessary to take off the gloves, sir."

Three television screens were bracketed onto the wall. One
displayed the empty stretch of corridor from the lift to the door
to the Vaults. Another revealed the second guard, lolling in the
Control Room, his legs up on the table in front of him. He was
reading a newspaper. The third screen showed the scene in the
anteroom.

"You must remove the gloves, sir," the guard repeated.

Hobart reached through the slit-pocket, finding the gun in his
jacket. His hand emerged, holding the thirty-two automatic. He
reached across the table, kicking the guard's foot away from the
panic-button.

The man's eyes bulged as he saw the gun. His arms shot up in
the air. His lips lost their color. Hobart herded him past the grille
into one of the cubicles.

"Down on your face or you're dead," Hobart snarled. He
ripped the phone from the wall.

The guard sank to his knees, still holding his arms high.
Hobart's shove sent the guard sprawling forward.

"Hands behind your back, slowly!" said Hobart.

He straddled the Asian, cut strips from the roll of industrial
tape in his bag and fastened the man's wrists and ankles. He
secured wrists and ankles with a trip loop and sealed the man's
mouth. The guard lay like a trussed chicken, his eyes filled with
terror. Hobart turned him on his side and closed the cubicle curtains on him.

He looked at his watch. Eight minutes had elapsed since they
had entered the building. Sweat was running down Hobart's ribcage. He glanced back at the TV control screens. The older guard
was still reading his newspaper. There was no surveillance of the
interior of the vaults. Hobart ran fifteen yards to the Control

Room, gun in hand. The Asian pounced on the phone as Hobart came in. Hobart yanked the cord from the wall.

"Down on your knees or I'll blow your brains out!" he yelled. His voice echoed along the corridor.

The guard obeyed slowly, a sly and resentful animal. His eyes assessed every move that Hobart made. Hobart trussed him and threw the switch on the television cameras. The three screens went blank. Buttons on the control panel identified their functions. VIDEO ROOF CAR PARK EXTERIOR ALARM CHELSEA POLICE STATION. Hobart turned them all off. He removed the surveillance cassette from the video machine. A box on the floor identified one cassette for each of the days that had elapsed in November. Hobart dropped all nine in the holdall. The guard's malevolent stare followed him from the room. The only sound was a low moaning from behind the curtained cubicle. He stuffed the automatic in the top of his trousers. There were six rows of lockers, thirty-five in each row. The face of the lock in front of him was identical to the mock-up made in the machine shop.

Hobart inserted the flat steel rod into the keyhole and applied the tripod to the front of the box, holding it in position with his chest. He turned the ratchet and felt the studs engage. Sweat was dripping into his eyes. He used his sleeve to wipe it away. He gave the ratchet another turn. The tripod was holding firm now, resisting pressure from inside the lock. The mechanism broke with a loud cracking sound. The barrel of the lock clattered onto the floor, the bit still jammed in the keyhole. Hobart hooked a finger into the empty space. The drawer slid out smoothly. It contained a large brown envelope. He looked at his watch again. Twenty-two minutes. He dropped the envelope into his bag, leaving the tripod and broken lock on the floor. He ran for the lift, the key card ready in his hand. The lift door slid back. Alarm bells started ringing as Hobart stepped inside the cab. The noise followed him down to the basement. Bells jangled inside and outside the building. A siren shrieked from the roof. Hobart ran for the wall, the card still in his hand. He rammed it into the slot in the wall. The massive steel door began rising. Daylight flooded into the basement.

Cameron's face was a blur in the car, his voice lost in the strident confusion. Hobart stuffed the key-card into the bag and aimed the bundle through the open car window. The Rover

started to move up the ramp. As Hobart reached for the handle of
the rear door, the older guard burst through the fire exit, carrying
a Winchester repeater. He fired as Hobart lifted the thirty-two.
Lead shot held in a tight pattern the size of a grapefruit. The full
force of the charge hit Hobart's head, removing his cap with most
of his brainpan. He dropped like a stone through water, his un-
fired gun clattering across the concrete floor.

The Rover roared up the ramp and turned towards Knightsbridge.

SEVEN

Cameron's only thought was to get out of there fast. He had no real judgement of what had happened, just the urge to run. He trod hard on the accelerator. The wheels gathered traction. The wail of the siren up on the roof of the Safe Deposit pursued him to the traffic-signals at the north end of Sloane Street. Green replaced red. The noise behind dwindled. Cameron swung the car left towards Kensington. A police cruiser was coming fast from the opposite direction, its warning light flashing. Cameron turned onto Queen's Gate, veered to the kerb and killed the motor. His fingers shook as he lit a cigarette, anxiously scanning the rearview mirror.

I do not believe this, he thought. *I simply do not believe it!*

He leaned forward and rested his head on the steering wheel, the cigarette burning between his fingers. He remembered the scene he had witnessed as a series of frenzied freeze-frames. Hobart bursting out of the lift, his long black raincoat flapping around his legs. The explosion of bone and brain tissue as the twelve-bore cartridge blew the enquiry agent's skull asunder. He straightened up suddenly and reached back for the bag that Hobart had thrown into the car. There was a pile of cassettes inside, the key-card that Hobart had used to get access and a large brown

envelope sealed with sticky tape. He stuffed the bag under his
seat. He had lost the sound of pursuit. The street was a dreary
wet waste, a Sunday afternoon desert. He flipped his smoke
through the window. His world had shrunk during the last thirty
minutes. He was still trying to make sense of what had happened.
He dismissed the story about Hobart's big chance, the woman
with a child, the whole bunch of shit that Hobart had laid on him.
The truth was that Hobart had conned him. On top of that, he'd
been involved in an armed stick-up, a raid on the Hans Security
Vaults with an accomplice whose head had been blown off. The
cassettes must have to do with surveillance. For all he knew his
face was on one of them. So what happened now, where did he
go, who could he turn to, the police? He saw himself sitting on a
chair under a bright light, one cop behind, another in front. Hostile faces. *Say what? Driving a car for a friend? Get out of here!* They'd
lock him up in a cell and throw the key as far as they could. And
who could argue with them? He didn't even know the name of
the lawyer Hobart was supposed to be working for. The implica-
tions grew with chilling clarity. The guy with the shotgun would
have taken the numbers of the license-plates. Hobart had given
Raven's address to the car-rental agency, produced his Canadian
Driving License. What he had to do was bury the rented car
somewhere and find some way of getting out of the goddam country.

He re-started the motor and drove down Queen's Gate, scanning each side of the wide thoroughfare. The first place the police
would look would be in the multi-storey car parks. Imperial College sprawled over six blocks, administration buildings, lecture
halls, lecture rooms and halls of residence. There was no sign of
life on the campus. He turned the Rover down a short service
road between grey stone buildings. A drop-bar gate in a chick-
enwire fence blocked the way. A wooden hut squatted behind the
fence. Beyond was an expanse of hardtop the size of a soccer field.
A few cars were parked there. Cameron ducked under the drop-
bar and walked across to the hut. It was locked. The bar lifted
freely. He drove the Rover onto the lot and parked it next to a
Volkswagen camper sporting an Australian flag. Cameron wiped
the steering wheel and door handles of the rented car with his
handkerchief. It was what he had seen them do on television. He
left the ignition keys in the lock and walked back to the hut, the

canvas bag under his arm. He ducked under the drop-bar again and hurried south towards Chelsea. A few more hours and students would be driving back to school. The Rover would be lost among a hundred or more vehicles.

He passed a phone-booth on Neville Terrace. He kept going. A phone-call was no way to break the kind of news he carried. A cab dropped him off at the bottom of Beaufort Street. The street lamps came on as he approached the flotilla of boats. The Ravens' car was parked outside Hank Lauterbach's gift shop. Cameron unlocked the door at the bottom of the stone steps, already thinking like a criminal would, suspicious and hunted. Music was playing as he walked along the deck to the sitting-room. He pushed the door open. It was warm inside. A record was playing on the machine. Kirstie was lying face-down on the carpet, her breasts propped on a couple of cushions. Her feet were bare, the rest of her body covered by a turquoise-blue track-suit. She looked up from the newspaper, pushing her hair from her eyes.

"Hi! You're back early. We didn't expect you until later. John's over on Hank Lauterbach's boat."

The sound of her voice made him want to weep. "Something came up," he said awkwardly. Anything rather than tell her the truth. He walked through to the guestroom and dropped the canvas bag on the floor. He slumped in a chair, staring out through the window at the grinding mooring-chains. The barge grumbled and groaned beneath him. Time passed. He had no idea how long. Someone tapped on the door. The handle turned. Kirstie came in. She sat on the side of the bed, looking at him.

"What's wrong?" she asked quietly.

The enormity of what had happened hit him again with sudden force. He shook his head, unwilling to meet her eyes.

"*Kirk!*" she insisted, tugging his shoulder, forcing him to face her. "This is *me!* What happened?"

"I'm in bad trouble, Kirstie. I have to talk to you both."

She rose without fuss and went through the bathroom into her bedroom.

He heard her pick up the phone and dial. "I think you'd better get back here, John. No, *now*, it's important."

She came back, put her arm around Cameron's shoulders and laid her cheek close to his.

He came to his feet, made to feel worse by this open display of loyalty.

"I need a drink," he said suddenly.

Kirstie followed him into the sitting room. She sat on the couch, watching as he stood at the drinks cupboard. Raven came in wearing a red track-suit. The Ravens usually jogged on Sundays.

Raven closed the door from the deck, looking from his wife to Cameron.

"What's going on?" he demanded.

"Kirk's got something to tell us," said Kirstie.

Cameron poured two fingers of scotch into a glass and swallowed it. He refilled his glass with a shaking hand, remaining standing with his back to the bookshelves and record-player.

"I've been lying to you both ever since I got here," he said. "There never was anyone who was going to give me an exhibition. Lies, the lot of it. That's not the reason I came to London. I came because I ran into this guy in Paris, someone called Henry Hobart. A private enquiry agent. He gave me this story about a rich woman with a child who was having problems with her husband. She was supposed to have been in Antigua with some guy. Pictures were taken and the husband got hold of them. He was suing for divorce and custody. Hobart was hired to get the pictures back. He said he needed my help." He spread his hands. "I was broke."

He finished his second drink. Raven sat next to his wife on the couch. Cameron forced himself to continue, each word a confession of gullibility.

"Anyway, the photographs. I don't have to tell you the kind they were. Hobart said the daughter was an heiress, that's why the parents were fighting. He said he was going to burgle the husband's locker in the Hans Security Vaults. The security guards were supposed to be in on the deal. They'd been paid off. The whole thing had been prearranged. More lies. He robbed the place with a gun this afternoon. One of the guards shot him dead. I drove the car."

He wiped his lips on the back of his hand and walked to the window.

"I'm going to try to pretend I heard none of all this," Raven said.

Kirstie swung round on him savagely. "For God's sake!" she cried.

She rose and stood beside Cameron. "You're shaking," she said.

Raven brushed past them both and filled a glass from the drinks cupboard. He swallowed a mouthful.

"*He's* shaking! What do you think I'm doing?" He buried his nose in his glass again. "You're sure that this other man's dead?"

"I was *there*," Cameron said. "Sitting in the car when he came out of the lift. The guard hit him with a pumpgun. They were close enough to shake hands. He's dead all right."

Cameron freed himself from Kirstie's grasp and made a gesture of bafflement.

"I can't explain. I mean, I'd known the guy for a couple of years. We'd have a drink whenever he came to Paris. Tell the truth, I figured him for a bit of a show-off. I didn't really know what he did. Industrial espionage, that's what he claimed. He was generous, lent me the money to pay my hotel bill." He shook his head at the mystery of it all. "Then the guy just went sideways on me."

A plume of hair sticking up at the back of Raven's head gave him the mien of an outraged rooster.

"You mean that you actually believed that balderdash?"

Cameron felt himself flush. The scar on his cheekbone was livid against his brick-red face. His words came impulsively. "What are you, infallible?"

Kirstie broke it up quickly. "Stop it, the pair of you! John doesn't mean what he's saying," she told Cameron.

"John means every bloody word that he's saying," said Raven. "You know how I feel about this man. This only proves me right."

"For God's sake," said his wife. "Kirk's a friend."

"Your friend, not mine," Raven said stubbornly. "Ok. We've just been told that our guest robbed a bank after lunch this afternoon. And he's on the run. What do you expect me to do about it?"

"The same as you'd do if he *was* one of your friends," Kirstie said tartly. "Have a heart for a start. I don't remember you moralizing when George Drury came running for help."

"George Drury . . ." He broke off and turned on the television set. The room filled with the announcer's bland tone.

". . . main points of the news again. The Prime Minister flies to Moscow." Raven nudged the volume control. "Two armed men attacked a Belgravia safety deposit vault early this afternoon. One remained in the car while his confederate overpowered the two guards at gunpoint. The thieves fled with the contents of a locker. One of the guards managed to free himself and gave chase. Shots were exchanged in the basement of the building and one of the robbers was fatally wounded. His accomplice escaped with the stolen property. A police spokesman said that the dead man had not yet been identified. Flooding continues . . ."

Raven turned off the set and looked at Cameron. "What did you do with the car?"

Cameron's eyes fixed on Kirstie. "It's in a car park in Imperial College. It's safe enough there. For the time being at least."

Raven shook his head. "I suppose you gave this address to the car-hire people, and your right name?"

Cameron nodded. "I saw no harm."

"No harm," Raven repeated. "The more I hear about this, the worse I feel. What happened to the stuff that you stole?"

Cameron heaved himself up. His movements seemed to have slowed. He fetched the bag from his bedroom and placed it on the couch next to Raven. Raven stacked the cassettes on the table under the lamp.

"Surveillance tapes. And you can bet that your picture's on them. What's this?" He held up the card-key.

"Hobart used it to get it into the car park," said Cameron. "And the lift."

Raven tore the sellotape from the envelope. He removed a Xeroxed copy of an invoice for £500,000. The writing alongside read "For professional services rendered." A photocopy of a check for six million, two hundred and thirty-seven French francs was clipped to the invoice. There were four passport-size photographs. The men portrayed appeared to be between twenty and thirty. All four wore short hair and baleful stares.

Raven put the documents back in the envelope. "Cyclops Security." It was the name on the invoice. "Did your friend ever mention that name?"

Cameron scowled. "You want to do me a favor, stop calling the bastard my friend. No, he didn't mention them. Nor did he say that he'd got a gun stuffed down the front of his pants."

Raven went through to the bedroom. They heard him talking on the phone.

"Patrick O'Callaghan," Kirstie said quietly. "He's our lawyer."

Cameron forced himself to look at her straight in the eye. "I didn't mean to do anything ugly," he told her.

"I know," she said patiently. "What I don't understand is how you could be such a fool. I mean, if you needed money, why not come to us? We'd have let you have it."

He shook his head. "Can't you see, Kirstie? How could I come to you, of all people?"

She frowned, disturbing the band of freckles that bridged her nose. She let her breath go.

"What are we going to *do* with you, Kirk?"

"Stick me on a rock-pile," he said morosely.

She came to life with new assurance. "John'll think of something. He'll help. He'd do it for me if not for you. He's a good man, Kirk. Believe me, I know."

Raven returned from the bedroom. He poured himself a scotch-and-water and sat down on the other couch, considering them. Kirstie rolled her eyes at the ceiling. Her husband paid no attention to her.

"Cyclops Security," he announced, "is run by someone called Paul Sheffield, an ex-major in 18 SAS. He only employs men who were in the regiment. You want my opinion, I'd say that you've just robbed his safety-deposit box."

Raven hauled up his right pants leg and inspected his calf. The varicotomy had left razor-thin scars on the back of his leg. Kirstie was buffing her nail on a cushion. "Patrick's met this chap Sheffield," Raven continued. "He says he's heavy. That is, in the line of business."

Cameron looked at him blankly. "What's that supposed to mean?"

"It means," Raven said behind uplifted finger, "that a man like Sheffield wouldn't take kindly to having his box robbed. And he'll know where to go for help if he needs it. Friends in high places, be sure of it. We won't only have the police to deal with, Sheffield's friends will be in on the act."

"You keep saying 'we.'" Cameron forced the words through the stop in his throat. "It's got nothing to do with you."

"You're either a fool or you're totally naive," Raven answered.

"You're staying here on the boat, you and Kirstie were at school together, old friends from way back. Added to which, I'm not popular with the police."

"That's right," Kirstie put in. "He declared war on them years ago. Crooked cops, cops with bad breath, you name it. I used to lose sleep worrying about it. I still do."

Cameron rose to his feet on impulse. "I got you into this. It's up to me to get you out of it. I'm going to turn myself in."

"For crissakes sit down," Raven said impatiently. "We've had enough heroics for the day. There isn't a cop on the Force who'd believe your story. And as soon as my name was mentioned, they'd know they were right. It isn't you that I'm worried about, it's Kirstie. She's had too much of this shit in the past." He turned to her. "Patrick's on his way round."

She looked relieved.

The Canadian was still staring at the floor between his feet when the entry buzzer sounded. Raven walked along the deck to meet his visitor. He came back, accompanied by a small man carrying a King Charles Spaniel.

"Maureen's playing bridge," the lawyer announced. "And Jamie hates being left by himself." He kissed Kirstie's cheek and nodded at Cameron.

Raven made the introductions. "Kirk Cameron, Patrick O'Callaghan." The two men shook hands. The lawyer was dressed completely in black. Corduroy trousers, pumps and a Levi Strauss top. The spaniel sniffed Raven's ankles, then jumped on the couch next to Kirstie. O'Callaghan opened one of the white painted cupboards and reached inside with the sureness of familiarity. He selected a cheroot from a box and lit it.

"I can't stay long," he said between small white clenched teeth. "I'm expecting a phone-call." He removed the cheroot from his mouth, holding it like a pen.

"This man here," Raven said, nodding at Cameron. "He's just robbed the Hans Security Vaults. The guy who was with him was killed."

The lawyer blew smoke at the cedarwood ceiling. "I don't think I should be listening to this," he said primly.

Raven started to say something. Kirstie silenced him.

"Let Kirk tell Patrick himself. Go ahead," she encouraged. "Explain how you got into all this in the first place."

Cameron made a visible effort to pull himself together. He seemed to have trouble in finding the right words.

"I was had," he said flatly. "And that's about the long and short of it."

"That's no good," Kirstie said. "You've got to explain."

Cameron looked at the backs of his fingers. "A guy I knew in Paris," he said, raising his head. "A private enquiry agent, industrial espionage, so he said. He was doing this thing in London. The work was highly confidential, something to do with a divorce case and custody. He needed someone he could trust to help out. Someone who would drive a car and keep his mouth shut. He offered me a couple of thousand pounds for a week's work. When you're as broke as I was, you don't apply logic to that kind of offer."

The lawyer glanced from one to another. "Let's get this straight. Why am I here? Am I being asked for legal advice or what?"

"Any sort of advice we can get," Raven answered.

O'Callaghan bared small white teeth. "I've been looking after your affairs for the past fourteen years, dragged along kicking and shouting for the most part. You have never listened to my advice. Or rarely."

"*Please*, Patrick!" Kirstie implored, putting her hand on his knee. "Kirk's an old friend. Do what you can for him, please!"

"The man got caught with his hand in the till," Raven said brusquely.

O'Callaghan removed his cheroot from his mouth. "What's the name of the one who was killed? I might know him. I use these people all the time."

"Henry Hobart," said Cameron. "I know that he's traded as Discreet Investigators, or Investigations."

O'Callaghan frowned. "Never heard of either."

"You don't read the *Police Gazette*," Raven said sourly.

Kirstie turned a baleful eye on him. "Why don't you shut up and let them do the talking?"

Raven removed himself to the bedroom. They heard him on the telephone there. By the time he returned, Cameron was through with his story. O'Callaghan was still on the couch, kneading the spaniel's ears, the cheroot smoke burning unheeded in the ashtray. Raven emptied the stolen bag onto the table. The lawyer laid the four photographs out like playing cards.

"*Not* a pretty sight," he said, shaking his head. "Not the class of person you'd want to meet in an alleyway, not even in broad daylight."

"That dog needs water," Kirstie said suddenly. She led the spaniel into the kitchen.

The lawyer read through the Xeroxed documents and replaced all the articles except the key-card.

"You say this got you into the car park and lift. Where did it come from?"

"Hobart had it," said Cameron. "He had this tool made to open the locker. That was left behind."

Raven closed his eyes and shook his head.

The lawyer said, "Let's look at the facts. If our friend here goes for trial, he'd certainly be indicted on the armed robbery charge. Anyone defending him would have a hard job convincing a jury that he's innocent. There *is* no real defense. His only chance is convincing the jury that he's a victim of circumstance. Juries are unpredictable."

Kirstie returned with the dog in time to catch the last few words. "What sort of chance are we talking about?"

The lawyer buried his fingers deep in the spaniel's ruff. He gave the question some thought before answering.

"Well, one thing's for sure. The story won't stand up as it is. A jury will see him as one of two things, a plausible rogue or an idiot. You'd have to build on the idiot image. Do that successfully and I'd say he'd have one chance in five of an acquittal."

Kirstie buried her face in her hands. "On the other hand, he can run," said O'Callaghan. "John knows more about that sort of thing than I do."

"Is that what you're recommending?" Raven asked.

The spaniel was snoring, curled in his master's lap. "It's the only thing that makes sense in my view," said O'Callaghan. "Let's face facts here. A serious crime has been committed, a man killed as a result of it. His confederate is an old friend of Kirstie's, a school friend no less. What we have to do is remember John's position in all this. The police don't like him. He's humiliated them too often. I *know*. They make it their business to tell me. An opportunity like this would be too good to miss. I don't think they'd go as far as bringing a conspiracy charge against John but "harboring a fugitive from justice" would be obvious. My advice is get our friend here off the boat as soon as possible." He nodded down at the bag. "And get rid of that too."

"I don't agree," Raven said forcefully. "A man's been killed because of what's in that bag. It's our insurance. If what you say is right about Sheffield having all this clout, he should be willing to do a deal."

"You're deranged," Kirstie snapped. "You asked Patrick here to give his advice. Ok, he's given it. But that's not enough for you. You want to extract the last ounce of drama."

Raven was fighting to control his temper. "The first time Kirk tries to leave the country legally he'll be nicked, no doubt about it. I'm trying to get this man Sheffield on our side."

"You can get Kirk out of the country," Kirstie argued. "You know the right people."

"I know lots of people," he said. "Most of them I wouldn't trust with that dog there!"

O'Callaghan rose, brushing the spaniel's hair from his trousers. Raven took an umbrella and the canvas bag. "I'll walk you home," he said.

The door slammed at the end of the gangway. Kirstie and Cameron looked at one another.

"I know what you're thinking," he challenged. "You're wishing that you'd never clapped eyes on me, right?"

"I just wish that you'd told us the truth," she said sadly. "That's as far as my brain will take me."

She walked into the kitchen, carrying the dirty glasses. For the next twenty minutes she busied herself preparing food for the three of them. Come hell or disaster, they still had to eat. When she returned to the sitting room, there was no sign of Cameron. She called his name. The only answer was the sound of the rain on the cedarwood roof. She ran through to the guest room. His suitcase was there, his return ticket to Paris, the keys to the boat. But his passport had gone from the dressing table.

She picked up the phone and dialed. O'Callaghan answered. "Let me talk to John," she said tightly.

Raven came on the line. "Get back here quickly," she said. "Kirk's disappeared."

"How do you mean, disappeared?"

"Just *gone!*" she insisted. "Flown the coop! He's doing what used to be called 'playing the white man.' And it's all thanks to you."

"I'm on my way," he said quickly.

She sat with the door to the deck ajar, waiting for Cameron to call.

EIGHT

Van Hall was standing at a library window, looking out along Kinnerton Street. Pigeons murmured on some sheltered ledge. Rain ran down the guttering. It was Sunday evening and the pub across the street was still dark. He closed the curtains and sat down at his desk. Saturday's mail lay unopened in front of him. He had just heard the news of the Hans Security Vaults robbery. He laid the facts out in his mind. It had happened before, the fabric of lies and deceit collapsing beneath him. He had learned to bluff and keep bluffing. Indecision was a form of weakness.

Hobart was dead but as yet unidentified. This would only be temporary. It was difficult these days for a corpse to remain anonymous. The police would be tying a tag to Hobart's toe any moment now. The good thing was that Hobart had never been to Kinnerton Street. The tape that the enquiry agent had made in Paris had been destroyed. There was nothing else that could link him to the dead man. Then he suddenly thought of it. *The card-key!* It bore the number of his locker and the name he had given when he rented the box. The news-reader had talked about the second man escaping with the stolen property. With any sort of luck the card-key would be among it. Van Hall opened a drawer aimlessly, closed it again. If worse came to worst, he would admit the association with Hobart. His brain wove the details. He'd say that he had employed Hobart on a few occasions, routine searches in government department files. He'd finally had to let Hobart go. The man had proved unreliable. If Hobart had taken the surveillance tapes as instructed, the danger was minimal. The main thing now was to get hold of Cameron before anyone else did. He must have gone straight to this boat he was staying on. There was no other place for him to go.

Van Hall lifted the phone and called Directory Enquiries. "The name is John Raven," van Hall said. "The address is a barge or a boat in Chelsea."

There was a pause as the operator put the details on her computer screen. Then she was back, trilling.

"I'm sorry, caller, that number is ex-directory."

He made a long-arm to the bottom bookshelf. The Voters List for Kensington and Chelsea gave him the address that he needed.

RAVEN John   ⎰Barge Albatross Chelsea Embankment SW 3
RAVEN Kirstie Arbela⎱

No telephone number was given.

He leafed through half-a-dozen reference books before he struck gold in the *Photographer's Yearbook.*

RAVEN Kirstie Arbela b. Toronto Canada April 1 1958 Educ. York Mills Academy For Young Ladies Toronto, Institut Selig, Château D'Oex Sur-Montreux Switzerland. Toronto School of Visual Arts. Work includes commissions for Gov. of Ontario. Vogue, Harpers, Paris Match, etc. Winner of Prix de Gaudry 1988, Joint medalist Fashion Award of New York 1988.
Home address   BARGE ALBATROSS CHELSEA EMBANKMENT SW 3 Tel 352 0043
Work   4 Lennart House Shepherds Market W.1. 355 7800

He replaced the books on the shelves, performing mundane acts with a new sense of urgency. He collected his car keys, and closed the door. The XJ6 growled in the narrow street. He drove west on King's Road and turned south on Beaufort Street. Battersea Park was closed for the night, the bridges a blurred tracery of lights spanning the river. He pulled the Jaguar to the kerb and surveyed the motley collection of boats. It was just after seven o'clock. A pub was open fifty yards away. Van Hall walked across. There was nobody in the bar except a young man behind the counter wearing a matelot top and a hoop earring. He lowered his newspaper. His accent was Etonian cockney.

"What can I get you, mate?"

"I'm looking for some people called Raven. The name of the boat is the *Albatross,* but I don't seem to be able to find it. Can you help at all?"

The young man pointed across van Hall's shoulder. "It's the last on the line. You can't miss it, the one with the long reddish top."

Van Hall raised a hand and walked back to the Jaguar. A flight of stone steps was cut in the granite embankment. Van Hall looked over the parapet. He had a clear view of the last two boats in the moorings. The name ALBATROSS was painted on the stern of the barge immediately below. A door opened onto the deck as he watched. Van Hall ran back to the Jaguar. Two men appeared at the head of the steps. The smaller of the two was carrying a spaniel, the other a canvas bag and umbrella that protected them both from the rain. They walked away quickly, turning south at the first corner.

Van Hall returned to the parapet and craned his head down at an angle. He could see the gangway at the foot of the steps beyond the door with its frieze of razorwire. Light streamed from the uncurtained windows on the river side of the superstructure, falling across the deck. Van Hall shifted position, the stone parapet scraping his chest. He could see through the window now. A man and a woman faced one another, apparently arguing. Van Hall heard nothing. Their mouths opened and shut as though in a silent movie. The woman broke off the conversation and vanished along a corridor. The man stayed where he was for a few seconds, disappeared in turn and was back within seconds wearing a nylon raincoat. Van Hall was behind the wheel of the Jaguar before the man reached the top of the steps. It was Cameron. Van Hall had no doubt of it. Van Hall went low in his seat as the Canadian hurried east on the opposite side of the Embankment. He had turned the corner onto Beaufort Street before van Hall had the Jaguar moving. Van Hall followed. A stretch of wet empty pavement welcomed him. A cab was pulling away from the kerb. The Canadian's red crewcut showed through the rear window. Van Hall went after the cab, keeping twenty yards behind. He was led through the featureless wastes of Pimlico. The cab stopped outside the Continental section of Victoria Station. Cameron appeared to know where he was going. He went in and out of the Hovercraft Reservation Office, leaning into the flame of a match as he surveyed the line of passengers waiting for the Calais boat train. A garbled message sounded in the speakers set high in the concourse rafters. The barrier lifted and the line of passengers verged forward.

The Canadian went out to the street, van Hall still behind him. It was a shabby neighborhood with purveyors of junk food, massage parlors, and shops selling souvenirs and cheap luggage. Seedy hotels catered for transients and the troubled in spirit. Cameron turned in under a lighted sign.

CLEAN ROOMS   COLOR TV
FRIENDLY ATMOSPHERE   CHILDREN WELCOME

The Canadian pushed through swing doors into the lobby. Van Hall was no more than a few feet behind. A woman was asleep in the small lobby, her feet resting on a suitcase fastened with a strap. Van Hall picked up a magazine. The girl at the desk took a good look at Cameron. She wore her hair in a beehive and pancake makeup.

"A room?" she said. "Haven't you got no luggage?"

Cameron jerked his head. "I checked it in at the station."

She yawned, making no effort to hide her boredom. It had been a long day. She ran the string of words together with no attempt at punctuation.

"That'll be sixteen fifty number eight on the second floor bathroom's at the end of the corridor all rooms got to be vacated before twelve o'clock noon or you're charged for another day no visitors after eight o'clock."

She made change for a twenty-pound note. Cameron walked up the stairs. Van Hall put his magazine down. The girl was studying Cameron's entry in the register. He had signed his name as Abbott.

"I'm with him," said van Hall, pointing up the stairs.

A light burned in the airless corridor. No sound came from number eight. Van Hall placed his mouth close to the door crack.

"It's a friend of Henry Hobart. Open up!"

The strip of light near the floor vanished. The door opened suddenly. Van Hall found himself dragged inside. The door was

kicked shut. Hands found his throat. He started to choke, struggling to remove the grip on his neck. He broke free, kneading the
flesh on his throat. An illuminated street sign outside threw pat-
terns of light on the ceiling. Cameron was standing between van
Hall and the door, his face set in hard planes.

"Just who the hell are you?" he asked.

Van Hall backed off, pointing across the bed at the phone. "We
can do one of two things. Either call the police or get out of here
fast. I'm your friend."

The Canadian cocked a menacing fist. "Don't give me that
shit!"

"It's true," said van Hall. "Hobart was working for me."

Cameron ran to the window, pulled back the curtain and
peeked down at the street. He switched on the light.

"Just who the hell are you?" he demanded, staring at van Hall.

"My name's van Hall. Come on, let's get out of here. We don't
have much time."

"I've already been conned left right and center," said Cameron.
"Why should I trust you?"

"Because I represent your only chance of safety," van Hall said
steadily. "The stuff you stole belongs to me. I want it back. I can
get you out of the country."

"I've heard it all before," Cameron said. He kept closing and
opening his fists, looking at van Hall. "Two thousand pounds for
a few days' driving. Wasn't that it? The woman with her goddam
daughter and husband. Asshole!"

"Listen to me," van Hall pleaded. "What's done's done. It's
what happens next that counts. The police are out there looking
for you. It won't take them long to find you. You need help, I'm
willing to provide it in return for my property."

Cameron moved his head from side to side. "I don't have your
goddam property."

"But you know where it is."

"I don't want other people involved," Cameron said.

Van Hall heard the despair in the Canadian's voice. "I know
who these people are," he urged. "You can call them from my
place. Tell them to get in a cab and meet you. You can be out of
the country within twenty-four hours. I guarantee it."

Both men jumped as the telephone rang. It was the woman
downstairs at the desk.

"It's gone eight o'clock. You'll have to get rid of your friend."

"I'm your only hope," said van Hall. "You won't last the night without me."

Cameron stared at him for fully a minute then picked up his raincoat.

"Let's go," he said suddenly.

NINE

Raven closed the gate to O'Callaghan's patio. He hurried back to the boat, umbrella held low, protecting himself from the driving rain. His leg was hurting again. He had spent the last twenty minutes listening as the lawyer talked to Detective-Inspector Forbes of the Special Branch. O'Callaghan occasionally dealt with immigration problems. According to Forbes, Cyclops Security was no subject for a Sunday evening chat. Forbes said that Cyclops was known to have contacts with departments of Her Majesty's Government. Nothing overt, of course, just the nod of the head when Cyclops had been asked to send high-explosive technicians to Sri Lanka, helicopter pilots to Guatemala. Sheffield himself was an enigma. The Inspector advised that if O'Callaghan was thinking of some sort of association, he should proceed with caution.

Kirstie was in the sitting room when Raven came in. He kicked off his sodden sneakers, put them in the kitchen sink with the umbrella and returned to the sitting room.

"Ok," he said. "Tell me what happened."

She frowned, looking at the end of the cigarette she was smoking.

"I already told you," she said. "He's gone!" She swung round, pointing in the direction of the bedrooms. "His bag's still there, so is his return ticket. He's taken his passport."

He looked at her accusingly. "Where can he go? He'll be nicked before morning. How could you let him do it?"

She laid a hand on her chest. "How could *I* let him do it! I didn't *know*, for God's sake! I was in the kitchen, fixing something for us to eat. I came back to find he was gone. He'd still be here if it hadn't been for you."

He blinked disbelievingly. "It turns out to be my fault, does it? Some low-rent Michelangelo robs a bloody bank and presto it's my fault."

Her face flared. "A man who'd just been through what Kirk had but you still had to make him grovel. Still had to make him feel cheap and disloyal, like a man who betrays his friends."

"Isn't that what he is?" her husband demanded.

She burst into tears. He caught her and held her tight, her face hidden against his chest. He dried her eyes with the sleeve of his track-suit and pulled her down on the couch beside him.

"Listen!" he said, forcing her to meet his look. "We both want to help him, right?"

She stared with red-eyed intransigence. "I will, no matter what happens. You'd better get that right at least."

"I understood, the very first day that I met you," he said patiently. "Nobody likes what they're doing. Patrick's going to put that bag in his safe in the morning. Do you think *he* needs all this crap?"

She drew a long breath and poured herself a glass of Perrier water. She sat down again. "So what happens now?" she asked quietly.

He reached for the phone and spoke for a couple of minutes. He replaced the phone on its rest. Jerry and Louise Soo lived down river in Wapping.

"I'll take the car. Jerry's going to wait in for me."

"I'll come too," she said promptly. "I don't want to be left on this boat on my own."

He pulled on a dry pair of sneakers, and collected his raincoat. "One of us has to stay here. Kirk might call any minute. I'll be home just as soon as I can."

He kissed her cool lips. Her tears never lasted for long. As soon as he had gone, she closed every curtain and locked and bolted the door to the deck. She changed into jeans and an old cableknit sweater of Raven's. His photograph stared at her from its silver frame in the bedroom. She had taken it on a fishing boat off the coast of Saint Lucia. It showed him standing with an arm wrapped around the mast, the sail billowing above him, his free hand shading his eyes. He was watching a hammerhead shark being winched aboard. She would never forget his look of pure pleasure. It was as if for one second he had dropped his habitual guard. She had made no comment. She already knew the answer. It wasn't the kill but the chase that excited him.

She slid from the end of the bed and went back into the sitting room. It was true, what she had told Raven earlier. At times like this she always felt nervous on the boat alone. A woman had been shot right here in this very room, shot dead by some cop with a deer rifle. She shivered at the memory, dragging down the sleeves of the sweater. She had long since come to terms with the fact that her husband was not as other men. Sometimes wondered if he would not have been better off with the sort of women he seemed to have hung out with. The bimbos that their cleaning lady remembered with so much enthusiasm. They seemed to have drifted in and out of John's life, seeking no more than they got, content as long as the affair lasted. None had left her mark on his soul and he rarely talked about them. At the beginning of their affair she had displayed curiosity, suggesting that he must have been in love many times before he met her. He agreed cheerfully, saying that he was still growing up.

She switched on the television in time to catch the news. The account of the Hans Security Vaults robbery had been scaled down to three minutes. The assailants were still unidentified. She silenced the set, wondering if Kirk had been watching. His stay on the boat had put their relationship in perspective. She loved Kirk in the way she had loved her dead brother. What mattered was that both had needed her. Kirk still did. It was almost eleven o'clock when the telephone rang. She lifted the handset with a feeling of apprehension.

It was Raven. "Has Kirk called?" he asked quickly.

"Not a word," she replied. "Did you watch the news?"

"I did," he said grimly. "And I didn't like it. Jerry knows nothing. What's worse is that people who do know aren't talking.

Louise went to bed. Jerry's still calling around trying to get news."

His voice sounded a thousand miles away. She wanted him there with her.

"When are you coming home?" she asked.

"Just as soon as I can. I told you, Jerry's still got his ear to the ground. I have to get off the line. Just stay by the phone. If anyone else but Kirk calls, you know nothing. Say that your husband's out, that he'll be back shortly."

"Ok," she replied.

what about dinner she was cooking

The call came while she was fixing a pastrami-on-rye in the kitchen. She picked up the phone on the dresser.

Cameron's voice broke. "Kirstie? You've got to help me, honey."

Anger and frustration welled into her voice. "Just what in hell do you suppose you are doing? What made you walk off the boat like that, like—like some thief in the night?"

"I had to," he said. "Look, there's no time to waste. Let me talk to John."

"He's out," she said curtly. He gave not one word of explanation or apology.

"Then you'll have to do it. That bag I had with me this afternoon, the one I brought back to the boat. I want you to grab a cab and take the bag to your studio. I'll explain everything when I see you. Can you be there in half-an-hour?"

"John's taken the car," she said. She was afraid to tell him that the bag was with Patrick O'Callaghan. She needed to talk to him, see him. "I'll be there as soon as I can," she said.

"Just *do* it for me," he urged. "You're the only friend I have left."

She replaced the receiver and ordered a radio-cab. She would have to keep him at the studio until John took over. Jerry Soo's number was engaged. She scribbled a note and put it on Raven's desk.

11.07 pm. Kirk just called. He's asked me to bring that bag to the studio, he's meeting me there. I didn't tell him that Patrick has it. Come to the studio QUICKLY. I'm going there now.

The cab took her to Curzon Street. She hurried through to the mews, the most expensive set of cobblestones in London, as

Raven called it. Property developers had transformed Victorian stables and quarters into one-bedroom residences. Kirstie's studio had once been a feed-store. Situated over a garage, it had been sectioned and south-light windows installed. Hers was the only non-residential premises in the mews. Lights showed in a few of the windows. Most of the people who lived there had not yet returned from the country. She unlocked the outside door and climbed the staircase. The previous owner had been an interior decorator. His taste was stamped on the dove-grey walls and carpeting, the Pompeian murals and fake-alabaster pillars. Kirstie had left most of it as it was. A birdseye maple table served as her desk in the reception area. There were batteries of professional lamps, a darkroom and an alcove fitted with a cooker and refrigerator. Edwardian finery spilled from theatrical baskets, relics of the period portraits Maggie Sanchez had modeled during the week.

Kirstie dialed Jerry Soo's number again. It was still engaged. She took the handset to the satin-upholstered couch and switched off the lights. She stood at a chink in the curtains with a clear view of the entrance into the mews from Curzon Street. Headlamps lit the front of the studio. They were extinguished immediately. Cameron emerged from the front of an XJ6 Jaguar and ran for the studio door, shielding his head from the rain with his mac. Kirstie's fingers found the button and released the downstairs door. She waited at the top of the stairs.

Cameron folded her close. "You're a princess," he said. He looked round sharply. "Where's the bag?"

She shut the door at the top of the stairs and stood with her back to it.

"Who is that man in the car?" she insisted.

He stepped back, redfaced, the scar livid on his cheekbone. His breath smelled of alcohol.

"It's someone who's helping me. Why didn't you bring the bag like I asked?"

"Why *didn't* I?" she repeated. "Because we don't have it any more, that's why. Patrick O'Callaghan's putting it in his safe."

He froze as though hit from behind then moved his head very slowly.

"I just don't believe this!" he cried, staring at her. "Do you realize what you've just done? You've blown my only chance of getting out of this shit that I'm in. How could you *do* that, you of all people?"

"Calm down," she soothed. "You should never have left the boat."

He drew a long breath and passed his hand across his forehead. "You and your goddam husband! You really are something else. Ok, I *know* I did wrong! That's why I skipped. I thought it would make things easier for you both. I didn't want you involved. But I don't seem able to win."

"Listen to me," she said calmly. "John doesn't *need* any of this, nobody does. But he's out there now, trying to help you. Are you going to tell me who that man is or not?"

His expression grew distant and hostile. "I'll tell you who he is, Kirstie. He's the guy who owns the stuff that was in that locker. And I'll tell you something else. He's the one person who can get me out of this bloody disaster and you've just pulled the plug on it."

He turned abruptly and ran down the stairway. For a second she thought he had gone again. Then two sets of feet sounded on the stairs.

The stranger was in his forties with a suntanned face and hands. He had smooth dark hair and the look of a man who lived well. He was wearing a navy-blue vicuna overcoat with its velvet collar upturned. The rest of his attire was equally expensive. His glance roved around the room and settled on Kirstie's handbag. He grabbed it and searched it thoroughly as she watched, too startled to offer objection. She just stood there disbelievingly until the spell broke.

"How dare you?" she said. "Kirk, why don't you do something?"

Cameron averted his gaze. The stranger handed the bag back to her. His voice was polite, his smile without warmth.

"Sit down, Mrs. Raven," he said, nodding across at the couch. Once she had sat down, he came a few paces closer to her. "I want you to listen to me very carefully. The bag that our friend here stole is my property. I want it back."

She raised her eyes. She had met many threats in her life. Hard-nosed cops from her husband's past, men who spoke with one foot in the doorway. None had spoken with this sort of menace. She could no longer control the shake in her fingers.

"We don't have the bag any longer," she said. "A friend took it. For safekeeping," she added.

The stranger moved closer again until he stood directly over her. "That property's mine," he said distinctly. "And I represent our friend here's only chance of freedom. I can have him on a boat to France within hours. That's no problem. On the other hand I can make sure that he spends the next ten years of his life on a rockpile or whatever convicts do in this country. The choice is yours, Mrs. Raven."

The shake in her hands had extended to her whole body. There was nothing that she could do about it. Cameron came to life.

"You're handling this the wrong way," he said to the stranger. "You're scaring the lady." His smile died under the other man's stare.

The stranger continued. "You're an intelligent woman, Mrs. Raven. I take it you want to help Kirk?"

She moved her head in assent.

"Then all you and your husband have to do is return what belongs to me. Then off you go to the sun or wherever. Just give the bag back. I take care of the rest. No problem."

She came to her feet in one swift movement, putting the table between the two men and herself. Anger replaced her fear.

"I want you out of here *now!*" she insisted. "You can get the hell out or I'll call the police." The phone was still on the couch on the far side of the table.

The stranger picked it up and offered it to her. "Be my guest," he invited.

She stayed where she was.

"Come on now," he said, putting the telephone down again. "We're on the same side, Mrs. Raven. Neither of us wants Kirk in trouble. We can work something out."

Cameron spoke as though he and Kirstie were alone in the room. "All my life I've been making mistakes," he said bitterly. "The biggest one was letting you go all those years ago. It's too late for that now but help me for old times' sake. You owe me that much at least."

His eyes held steadily under her inspection, moving her to compassion. She hated his misery, the change in him.

"I won't do a thing behind John's back," she said stubbornly.

The stranger broke in quickly. "There's no need for that, Mrs.

Raven. Look, all you have to do is pick up the phone and call your husband. We can all sit down and discuss this thing sensibly."

She shook her head, torn between her two loyalties. "You don't know my husband."

The stranger consulted his watch. "We don't have much time. Do you know how to get hold of him?"

His slate-colored eyes had the calculation of a crocodile. She avoided them.

"He went out and that's all I know," she said.

He scribbled and passed a piece of paper to her. "Tell him to call this number the moment he gets back. It doesn't matter how late, I'll be there."

For a moment she thought he was telling her that she was leaving with Cameron. The stranger's look disabused her.

"Kirk can stay here," she urged. She glanced around the room, making up some kind of bed in her mind. "He'll be safe. I'm the only one with the keys."

The stranger patted her arm, giving his saurian smile. "He'll be safer with me, Mrs. Raven. You go back to the boat. Tell your husband that I'll be waiting for his call."

She picked up her handbag. Cameron's glance pleaded with her.

"This doesn't make sense," she objected. "I don't even know your name."

"Call me Van," said the stranger. "I'm sure your husband and I can do business together. Goodbye, Mrs. Raven."

She heard them go down the stairs. Headlamps flared against the drawn curtains. The Jaguar purred and was gone. It was nearly midnight. A despatcher promised a radio-cab in ten minutes. She turned off the lights and waited downstairs in the doorway, sheltering from the rain and thinking of Cameron. It was the first time she had seen him afraid and she doubted she would ever forget it. She made a conscious act of faith, telling herself that everything would come right. John would see to it.

The cab dropped her in front of the boat. The Fiesta was back in the alleyway. She put her key in the sitting room door. The bolt held it fast on the inside. She rapped on the lighted window, huddled under the overflowing guttering. The bolt was withdrawn. Raven hurried her inside. She stripped off her coat and beret and shook her hair loose. Her voice filled with tears and frustration.

"What *kept* you, for God's sake?"

He looked at her closely and drew her across to the couch. "Sit down," he said. "I'll fix you a drink."

"I don't *want* a drink," she said, sinking down on the cushions. "He was there, John, standing in front of me, and I couldn't hold on to him."

He sat down beside her and took her hand. "I only got home five minutes ago. I called the studio the moment I saw your note. But you'd already left. Tell me what happened."

She shook her head helplessly, still unable to think clearly. "I got there first then this car arrived. Kirk came upstairs, the driver stayed in the car. Kirk was strange. I mean weird. He'd been drinking but that wasn't it. He was scared, John. And I've never seen Kirk scared in my life before."

Raven moved his shoulders. "A man in his position, he's got reason to be scared. What did he say?" The top of his track-suit was mapped with soy-sauce stains. Louise Soo must have fed him.

"He wanted that stuff that he stole, the stuff in the bag. He went berserk when I told him we hadn't got it. He accused me of trying to destroy him. Then he brought this other man up from the car. Van, he said his name was. He seemed to know everything about us. You, me, the boat. Everything. He said the stuff Kirk stole from the vault belonged to him. He wants it back."

"Describe him," said Raven.

Kirstie made an effort to remember. "In his forties, suntanned. Well-dressed and driving an XJ6. He speaks English perfectly but I get the impression that it isn't his mother tongue."

Raven weighed every word. "Did he say that the locker was his?"

She shook her head. "That wasn't mentioned. Just the fact that the property belonged to him. That and he wants it back. If we do that, he'll take care of the rest. Get Kirk safely out of the country and so forth. Most of the time, he's smiling. He makes me break out in a cold sweat, John. He's evil." She took the piece of paper from her handbag and gave it to him. "This is the number to call. He said that he'll be there waiting for an answer."

Raven read the prefix on the paper. "Three eight eight. That's somewhere near Regent's Park. Not a great deal to go on."

She was suddenly tired and drained of emotion. Her voice betrayed it. "I'm not just some bimbo, John. Don't patronize me."

Their eyes clashed in the giltframed mirror. "What the hell are you talking about?" he asked. "We're in a mess and I'm doing my utmost to help. Are you blaming *me* for what's happened?"

She sat up, her back very straight. The door and windows were shut, the boat warm under the rain. Any other Sunday night they would have been fast asleep at this hour.

She smoothed an eyebrow with her finger. What little makeup she wore was blurred.

"I blame no-one," she said, shaking her head. "A friend needs help and that's all I know."

"That's what we're trying to do," Raven said. "Provide help. Just how much does Kirk's future mean to you?"

The truth came tumbling out. "It isn't just Kirk, John. It's you and it's me. You said it earlier. Patrick said it and I'll bet that Jerry Soo said it. What happens to Kirk affects all three of us."

"Why won't you answer my question?" he insisted.

She looked at him sadly. "What you really want to know is whether I'm in love with Kirk Cameron. The answer is no. He came back into my life after all those years and I wish that he hadn't. The point is that he did. You're the only man that I love but I can't and won't walk away from Kirk now."

"I wouldn't expect you to," Raven said. "Come to that, I wish that we'd never gone to Paris last week but we did. I had a long talk with Jerry. His leave doesn't finish until tomorrow so he hasn't been into the office yet. All the people he's called claim they know nothing about the Hans Security Vaults robbery. There are no more media statements. Just a complete silence. That means one of two things. The police don't know what the hell they're doing or someone upstairs has put a block on the story. Jerry's considered opinion is that we should take a long trip, to Australia for preference."

"And is that what you want to do?" she asked quietly.

"No it isn't," said Raven. "I want Kirk out of the country, not us. None of this really happened, Kirstie. If anyone asks, we say yes we knew Kirk. You were at school with him. We ran into him in Paris, and all of that. He told us he was coming to London to arrange an exhibition of his paintings. He left the boat this morning on his way back to France and that's the last we saw of him."

He reached for the phone and dialed Patrick O'Callaghan's number. It took a long time to answer. The lawyer made no secret of his displeasure.

"Who is this," he growled.

"It's me," Raven said.

"I should have known," said the lawyer. "Have you any idea what time it is?"

Raven glanced at the clock on his desk. "I make it twenty-five minutes to one."

"Exactly. And that means that I was fast asleep. Maureen still is. What the hell do you want?"

"Something just came up. I need that bag back, Patrick."

"You want it back, come and get it," said the lawyer. "And the sooner the better."

"I'll be round in five," Raven said. He replaced the handset before O'Callaghan could change his mind.

"He didn't sound too pleased," Raven said. "I'm going round there."

She reached for her Burberry. "This time I come too. I'll wait in the car."

The rainfall outside continued. They made a dash across the road, huddled under the umbrella. Raven was carrying Cameron's overnight bag. They drove west along the Embankment. The pub was shut for the night. One car without lights stood under the dripping trees on the forecourt. The road narrowed near the bend to King's Road. Raven pulled to the kerb. He threw Cameron's bag over the parapet. It broke the surface of the water and sank without trace.

Raven drove around the corner to Old Church Street. Kirstie sat muffled in her raincoat collar beside him. He stopped in front of the O'Callaghans' house and unfastened his seatbelt.

"If I can't do this to Patrick, then who the hell can?" He rang the bell at the side of the ornamental iron gate that guarded the patio. Rain dripped on Maureen O'Callaghan's Japanese motor car. A lamp disguised as a coach lantern came on above the front door of the house. The door opened a crack, showing the life-size statue of Saint Francis standing in the hallway. The lawyer peered through the crack, the bag from the Vaults in his hand, blocking the entrance into the house.

"Just take it and go!" said the lawyer, giving Raven the bag. "I hope you know what you're doing."

"So do I," Raven said. The door closed and the light went out.

It was dark and the street was awash. Kirstie still crouched on the front seat, staring out through the windshield. They drove back along the Embankment and into the cul-de-sac.

He bent down to pick the bag up from the floor, then stopped when he saw the look on her face.

"What's the matter?" he asked.

She reached for the door-catch. "There was a car parked outside the pub when we drove past. An XJ6. It isn't there now."

"You're hallucinating," he said, avoiding her eyes. He knew that she was right.

They made a run for the opposite side of the Embankment and hurried down the flight of stone steps. Raven bolted the door and drew all the curtains. He dialed the number on the slip of paper Kirstie had given him. A man's voice answered.

"I'd like to speak to Van," Raven said.

"This is Van." The voice was as he had expected it to be from Kirstie's description.

"You talked to my wife," Raven said carefully. "I'm ready to deal but there's a difficulty about the delivery. It's impossible before Tuesday."

"Why Tuesday?"

"Because that's the way it has to be. The man who has what you want has been called to the country. There's been a death in the family. It's impossible for me to get hold of him until he comes back."

"How many people know of our arrangement?"

"Just you, Kirk, my wife and myself. The envelope in the bag is still sealed. My lawyer's got no more idea what's in it than I have."

"You say *lawyer?*" The voice sharpened. "I hope we're not playing games here, Mister Raven."

"Tuesday afternoon," Raven promised. "Late afternoon. Delivered wherever you want. You can rely on me."

He put the phone down and looked at his wife. She put the mug of cocoa down on the table.

"I don't know why you don't just give him the bag." Raven took a sip from her mug. "I think he's lying. I don't believe that stuff is his. On top of that, once he's got the bag, we've got nothing to bargain with."

"Kirk seems to trust him," said Kirstie.

Raven stood on his feet. "I wouldn't say Kirk's the best judge of human nature," he said. "Give me a hand with the freezer."

They went into the kitchen. He took a ball of twine from a drawer in the dresser. Together they dragged the heavy freezer away from the wall, revealing the trapdoor set in the floor. He raised the flap and found the switch that illuminated the hold. He carried the bag down the ladder and lifted a second hatch in the floor. Bilge water sloshed below, oily and evil-smelling. He cut off a length of twine and tied a double-reef knot in it. He used the line to suspend the bag over the bilge. It hung there, swaying with the movement of the boat. He lowered the hatch again. His burglar tools and unlicensed gun had been hidden down here for years without discovery. They wrestled the freezer back in position. Kirstie jumped as a loud report came from the street overhead.

"This thing's getting to us. It's just a car back-firing," he said. "Let's go to bed."

They lay like spoons in the darkness, rain lashing the windows. His arms were round her naked body from behind, his face buried in her hair. She stirred in his close embrace.

"Are you sure?" she murmured.

"Sure about what?" He was almost asleep.

She twisted quickly, attempting to read his face in the twilight. "Sure about us."

He felt the beat of her heart close to his chest. "Sure and certain," he said.

TEN

It was just after ten o'clock on Monday morning. Paul Sheffield's telephone number had been busy since eight o'clock. A half-pint mug of strong Salvadorean coffee perched on a table near the window. The rain had stopped and the sash was lowered, letting in the cool damp air. Sheffield finished dressing. The suit he had chosen was of grey tweed herringbone with unpadded shoulders and cuffs on the sleeves. Most of his suits had been made by a Savile Row tailor after Sheffield's discharge from the army. He tied the usual Windsor knot in the pink silk cravat and fished his glass eye from the saline solution. A shot from a Bogside sniper armed with an Armalite had removed the genuine article. The exploit had earned Sheffield the Military Cross and an honorable discharge from the army. Three months later he started Cyclops Security. His sense of humor was wry and private. His choice of a glass eye with a black iris was typical. His good eye was blue. The shock effect created gave him satisfaction. Sheffield despised eyepatches as being suitable only for pirates and models in shirt advertisements.

He belted his old camelhair overcoat and donned a much-abused brown trilby hat. He left the house and crossed Holland Park Road to the park gates. He climbed the rise to where Joe

Fraser sat on a bench, his hands thrust deep in the pockets of his black overcoat. He wore no hat. His features were cast in a serious mould, a high forehead occupying the space between greying hair and eyebrows. He was fifty-four years old, a detective-inspector in the Special Branch and attached to MI 5 Operational.

Sheffield placed his open newspaper on the damp bench and sat on it, his back to the peacocks strutting behind the iron railings.

"Glad you could come," Sheffield said pleasantly, his good eye roving. A solitary nanny was pushing a perambulator. It was too early for the professional bench-sitters.

"I'm here unofficially," Fraser said with the burr of his native Galloway. He cracked a Polo mint between his teeth, using his molars.

"I understand that," Sheffield said impatiently. "So what's happening?"

Fraser turned his head sideways. "Well, in the first place they know that your safety-deposit box was burgled."

"How do they know that?"

Fraser spread his hands. "There's a query about the nature of your loss. They're wondering what you had in the box."

"And what *do* they think?"

Fraser smiled like a horse about to neigh, withdrawing his long upper lip from his teeth.

"They don't know. That's what's pissing them off. They know it spells trouble but nobody's been able to spell."

"Bits and pieces," Sheffield said vaguely. "Things that could be embarrassing in the wrong hands. *Would* be," he emphasized.

Fraser transferred his gaze from his neatly shod feet to a pile of dead leaves.

"I'm giving you as much as I've got, Paul."

Sheffield nodded. "Do they know who the dead man is?"

"Not a clue. They took his dabs but there's no record. Forensic's been poking around in his mouth but that didn't help. They've had more luck with the other fellow. Kensington found the getaway car at six o'clock this morning, up there behind Imperial College. It was an Avis Rental machine booked out to a Canadian giving an address in Chelsea."

"And the name and address were false, of course," Sheffield said.

"Wrong," said Fraser. "The man's name is Kirk Cameron. He

produced an Ontario driving-license when he hired the car. Passport Control's got him entering the country from Paris last Monday. The name of the people he's staying with is Raven. They live
on a boat in Chelsea."

Sheffield frowned. "That doesn't make sense for a start. Who in
his right mind rents a car to use in a stickup and then gives his
right name and address?"

"Kirk Cameron." Fraser spread his hands again. "The press are
sniffing around but there's a D-Notice out on the story. However,
there is an interesting aspect."

He reached into his overcoat pocket and placed a folded piece
of paper on the bench between them. Sheffield opened the computer printout. It dealt with the service record of John Raven in
the Metropolitan Police. Sheffield read it through and whistled
softly.

"The man sounds like a menace. What's the matter with him?"

"I never knew him." Fraser's mouth expressed disapproval.
"He resigned ten or twelve years ago. I was still out in the sticks.
They say he was offered retirement but he insisted on resignation. Told them to stuff his pension and benefits. He's got private
money and his wife's a professional photographer. He's been
causing trouble ever since he left the Force. Several ex-cops are
cracking rocks because of Mister Raven. What I hear, if he was a
horse it'd take two men and a boy to ride him." He reached across
and retrieved the printout. "Like I said, I'm here unofficially."

"You already made your point," Sheffield said.

"The thing is," Fraser said, "there's something I'm supposed to
tell you. The people up on the fifth floor are keeping this thing
under wraps for one week from today. After that . . ." He
spread his hands again.

Sheffield stared, his glass eye fixed. "What the hell's that supposed to mean?"

"They're pulling the plug on you, Paul," Fraser said.

"Nice people," said Sheffield. "The salt of the earth."

Fraser nodded morosely. "It isn't the Branch, it's the F.O.
They're saying it's your shit, not theirs, and they want you to get
rid of it. They don't care much how."

"Then why interfere in the first place?" said Sheffield.

"Because you notified the duty officer yesterday evening. The
man was sitting there quietly reading page three of the Sunday

newspaper, all those bums and tits. 'Sensitive documents,' you said. I've seen a copy of the report."

Sheffield considered the other man closely. "If nobody's supposed to know anything, how come you know so much, Joe?"

Fraser lifted his shoulders. "I'm their number one errand-boy."

"Who's in charge of this investigation?" Sheffield said.

"Commander Mathew Drummond, our resident expert on the psychological approach to crime detection. And an asshole to boot."

"Ok," said Sheffield. "If that's what they want. Tell them to get off my back and I'll deal with this in my own way."

Fraser pushed himself up from the bench. "I'd better warn you, Paul, this Drummond takes himself seriously.

"So do I," Sheffield said. "I'll talk to you."

ELEVEN

The telephone rang. Raven reached from the bed, picked up the handset and leaned back into the nest of pillows."

"Hello!"

"It's me," said Jerry Soo. "Are you alone?"

"My toes curl up every time I hear that question," said Raven. "Yes, I'm alone. Kirstie's gone to the studio. What can I do for you?"

Traffic noise in the background indicated that the detective-superintendent was using a carphone.

"I've just left the office. Someone from Special Branch pulled your file from Admin last night. The guy who signed the book is an inspector called Fraser. They've still got it up there on the fifth floor."

"My *file!*" Raven repeated. "I've been off the Force for eleven years, Jerry!"

The background noise lessened. The car Soo was traveling in was held at the lights.

"Don't be naive," he said. "They know who you are and they know that Cameron's staying with you."

"*Was,*" Raven corrected. "He's gone. I was hoping you might have news of him."

"Not a word," said the Hong Kong–born cop. "And there won't be, now that the Branch has taken over. The man in charge is Commander Drummond. Remember that name. He's an asshole."

"Fuck him," said Raven.

"Brave words," answered Soo. "Another thing, you'd better be careful when you talk on the phone from now on. They've got someone over at Horseferry Road, making an application to bug your line. And watch out when you use a phone in the neighborhood. Make it a couple of miles away. They want your friend badly."

"So do I," Raven said.

"Well, you just take care now," warned Soo. A horn blared and the dialogue ended.

Raven swung his legs to the floor. The news that his phone was about to be tapped was predictable. It was no more than he had expected. He knew the procedure of old. A ranking police officer attended in front of a magistrate either before or after the normal day's business. The applications were always made in private. There was no record of any such request being refused.

He opened the door to the deck. It was damp and grey outside under an overcast sky. He dropped the kitchen scraps over the side, making sure that the ducks beat the seagulls to it. He knew little about the Special Branch, nothing of Commander Drummond. Raven had been on a marksmanship course once with a couple of Special Branch officers assigned to VIP protection. He'd found them professional, closemouthed and clannish. There was something like three thousand of them at full strength, stationed all over the country. They manned major ports, attended political rallies and worked closely with the security services.

Raven walked back to the bedroom. He had to be careful not to involve Jerry Soo any further. The Chinese man had come up the hard way, from a basket left on the steps of the Methodist Memorial Hospital in Hong Kong to a career on the Metropolitan Police Force. At the age of forty-five, Soo was a detective-superintendent working out of C2, Case Papers and Correspondence. He was much liked and respected, and the last thing he needed was to be linked with someone in Raven's plight.

The door buzzer caught Raven's attention. A voice sounded in the speak-box.

"John Walters, Immigration Service. Is Mrs. Raven there, please?"

"I'm afraid she's not available at the moment," Raven said. "May I be of help? I'm her husband."

"If you wouldn't mind, sir. It's just a routine matter."

Raven pressed the button that released the door at the foot of the steps and went out to meet his visitor. A man appeared on the gangway. His clothes were of nondescript cut and material and he walked as though he had stones in his shoes. A thickish mustache curled down over the ends of his mouth. He extended his hand in greeting and followed Raven into the sitting room, clucking approval. He walked to the end of the long room and backed off, admiring the view.

"Now this *is* really something!" he said. He shook his head and stared again through the panoramic window. "I'll bet you can see halfway down the river on a clear day!"

"Not quite," said Raven. "There are too many bends. Why don't you take a seat?" He indicated the nearer couch.

The visitor dropped his briefcase next to the book that Kirstie was reading.

"I've always dreamed of living somewhere like this," he announced. "It's a lot more romantic than Sutton, let me tell you."

He opened his briefcase and extracted a few sheets of typescript, stapled together, and placed a pair of reading spectacles on his nose.

"I understand that you have a Mister Kirk Cameron staying here with you?" he asked, looking up.

"He *was* staying," Raven said easily. "He went back to France yesterday morning. That's where he lives."

Walters pursed his lips. "Are you sure about that?"

"As far as I know," Raven said. "I thought it was my wife that you wanted to see."

"I wanted a word with them both as a matter of fact," Walters said.

Raven smiled. "It doesn't seem to be your day then, does it?"

Walters touched his mustache. "Left yesterday morning, you say."

Raven cocked his head. "That's right. He had his bag and his passport with him. He said he was going to Heathrow. We assumed that he was."

Walters returned the typescript to his briefcase. "The problem is that there's no record of Mister Cameron having left the country."

A chuckle was not one of Raven's accomplishments, but he did his best.

"Why do you call it a problem?"

"Just a manner of speaking," said Walters. He was on his feet and strolling down the corridor before Raven could stop him. The Immigration official walked to the end, glanced into both bedrooms and walked to the kitchen.

"Now this is sheer heaven," he said. "I can imagine you lucky people on a summer's day, out there on deck with a jug of lemonade. Or something stronger." He knocked his heel on the floor, his voice curious. "What's under this?"

"Bilge," Raven said. Scuff-marks showed on the linoleum where the freezer had been dragged across the floor.

"Of course," Walters said, smiling. "There'd have to be bilge, wouldn't there?"

He hobbled back to the sitting room and resumed his place on the couch. His manner grew confidential.

"The real reason I'm here, Mister Raven, is that Mister Cameron gave your wife's name and this address to the Immigration officer at Heathrow."

"That's right," agreed Raven. "We were over in Paris last weekend and ran into him. He's an old friend of my wife's and we offered him a bed."

"And very nice, too," approved Walters. "The thing is, we seem to have lost all trace of him."

Raven smiled. "Kirk's an artist. A painter. They seem to have different rules. He might have met someone he knew. Decided to stay."

"You mean a young lady?" said Walters. "Someone he wouldn't want your wife to know about?"

Raven's reply gathered gravel. "Let's get something straight here. It's of no concern to my wife who Cameron sees or stays with. He was our guest for six days and that's all there is to it. He had a set of keys and he came and went as he pleased. We don't ask questions of people who stay with us. I'm sorry, Mister Walters, but I can't help you further." He opened the door to the deck.

Walters heaved himself up. "Let me leave you my card. If Mister Cameron should be in touch, ask him to give me a ring on this number. As I said, it's purely an administrative matter. If we can get it sorted out here and now, he'll save himself trouble on any other trip he may want to make to the UK."

Raven placed the card in the tray on his desk. "If he does call, I'll tell him. Goodbye, Mister Walters."

He closed the door to the deck. Shooting the bolt was a purely reflexive action. He sat on the couch with the card in his hand.

IMMIGRATION AND NATIONALITY DEPARTMENT
LUNAR HOUSE CROYDON SURREY

The name "John Walters" and a telephone number had been penciled in below. Raven heard the door to the steps bang. He dialed the telephone number on the card. A recorded voice said, "You are being held in a queue. Calls will be answered in rotation. Please wait until you hear a ringing tone."

The wait was no longer than seconds. A woman spoke. "Immigration and Nationality Department, may I help you?"

"I've been told to get in touch with a Mister Walters, John Walters," said Raven. "There was an extension number but I seem to have lost his card."

"And your name is?"

"John Raven."

"If you'll hold, I'll make some enquiries." She was back in short time. I'm sorry, caller, but I'm unable to locate a Mister John Walters."

It was ten minutes or more when the telephone rang again. Raven was in the kitchen making coffee. He answered.

A man came on the line, his voice briskly efficient. "May I talk to Mister Raven please? This is the Department of Immigration and Nationality. Inspector Surtees speaking."

"Speaking," said Raven.

"Ah yes, Mister Raven, good morning. I understand you just called our office asking for Inspector Walters?"

"That's right. The girl said she didn't know him."

The man chuckled in apology. "Sorry about that, Mister Raven. She's new and got hold of the wrong personnel line. I'm afraid that Inspector Walters is out of the office at the moment. Can I get him to call you back later?"

"Don't bother," said Raven. "It's just that we had an arrangement—I lost his card and wanted to be sure that I had the right number."

He stood in front of the kitchen dresser, staring at the cradled phone for some time. His phone was unlisted. Walters could have read the number on the disk on the receiver. The digits on the card Walters had left must refer to a service number used by the Special Branch. It would ring out in Croydon and be transferred to the Yard. They were wasting no time.

Raven left the boat shortly after three o'clock. Kirstie had taken the Ford to the studio. A backlog of traffic stuttered along the Embankment, horns blaring, sprinting whenever the signals changed. A passing cab stopped and lifted Raven to Upper Berkeley Street. Raven made his way up to the second floor. O'Callaghan's secretary smiled a greeting. She and Raven were on first name terms.

"He's expecting you," she said, nodding at the door opposite.

The lawyer was sitting behind his desk. The room was the usual shambles. The table set against the end wall was topheavy with deed-boxes piled one upon the other. Every inch of space carried its load of documents. The floor was strewn with briefs tied with pink tape. Correspondence littered the top of the desk. Most of it was unopened. A tailcoat and white piqué waistcoat hung in a dry-cleaner's plastic sheath on the back of the door. The King Charles spaniel snored on a chair.

Raven cleared a space and straddled a chair, forearms leaning on the backrest.

"I've got a busy afternoon coming up," said the lawyer. "I can let you have halfnhour."

"I had a visit this morning," said Raven. "Someone claiming to be from the Immigration Service. He didn't turn in a very good performance but then he wasn't trying too hard. I think all he wanted was to see and be seen. Special Branch, Patrick."

O'Callaghan winced as though a dental drill had hit on a nerve. He rose, went to the window and stared down at the street. It was raining again.

"I hope you weren't followed," he said nervously.

"What difference could it make?" Raven said. "Everyone

knows you're my lawyer. Anyway, why *wouldn't* I be coming to see you?"

"This is different," said O'Callaghan. "I try to keep this kind of thing away from the office." He resumed his seat.

The fax machine clattered in the outer office. "Last night," said Raven, "when I got back from walking you home. Cameron had taken off."

"Taken off for where?" the lawyer demanded.

"How the hell do I know?" said Raven. The question and lack of an answer stressed his frustration. "He skipped while Kirstie was in the kitchen. He left the keys to the boat in his room with his bag and vanished into the night."

The lawyer reached for the box of Havanas. "You didn't say anything to me when you came to collect the bag."

"It wasn't the moment," said Raven. "You weren't in the best frame of mind."

O'Callaghan guillotined one end of the cigar he had chosen. He struck a match, eyes half-closed as the smoke rose.

"There's nothing about his arrest on the news."

"That's because he hasn't *been* arrested. And if he is, you'll hear nothing about it. There's a D-Notice out on the whole affair. Cameron called the boat when I was over at Jerry Soo's. Kirstie talked to him. He wanted her to meet him at the studio and bring that bag of stuff to her. She told him that we no longer had it."

The lawyer pulled an anxious face. "I hope that my name wasn't mentioned."

"Kirstie's no good when it comes to subterfuge," Raven said. "In any case, she's been in a state of near-shock since yesterday. You know her by now, Patrick. She'll go on doing whatever she can to protect Cameron. That's the problem."

O'Callaghan aimed smoke at the ceiling. "So what happened? I mean, did she go to the studio or what?"

"She went," Raven said. "Cameron turned up with this other guy who claims that the stuff that was stolen belongs to him. If we give it back, he says, he can get Cameron safely out of the country. He claims that'll be an end to it. The whole thing will die a natural death, no unpleasantness for anyone. It sounds like bullshit to me."

"Have you any idea who this man is?" asked the lawyer.

Raven moved his head from side to side. "He gave the name

'Van.' He left a telephone number with Kirstie. I called. He said the same thing to me as he had to her. He said the stuff that Cameron stole belongs to him. He said that if we'll return it he'll guarantee to land Cameron safely in France."

"And if you don't?"

"He didn't say."

"But you don't believe him?" the lawyer insisted.

"I'll tell you what I believe," Raven said. "I believe he needs those documents. For whatever reason. Cameron's with him. They both seem quite happy with the arrangement. The guy's given me until tomorrow night to produce the goods."

The lawyer removed a shred of tobacco from his lower lip. "I don't want to know where that bag is, John," he warned. My advice to you is distance yourself from it just as soon as you can. For once in your life you're blameless—try to keep it that way. Think about Kirstie."

"You get excited, your eyebrows go up and down," Raven admonished. "I *am* thinking of Kirstie. If I don't help Cameron, she'll never forgive me."

"You're out of your depth," said the lawyer. "Or haven't you realized it?"

"It's entered my mind," Raven admitted.

"These people don't play your rules, John," O'Callaghan said. "They have their own. You're not dealing with the sort of villains that you and I know. Their values are totally different. They don't care about their old mothers or Christmas. These are bad, bad people, my friend."

"I'm a quick learner," said Raven.

The lawyer decided to persevere. "You're—what is it—forty-three years old. Cameron is *not* your responsibility. Any more than he's Kirstie's. Friendship isn't suicide. My advice to you, not that you'll take it, is to get on a plane for Tahiti with Kirstie."

"I can't *do* that," Raven said obstinately.

"You mean that you *won't* do it," said O'Callaghan.

Raven hung over the back of the chair behind the pointing finger. "Maybe *you* should be taking a holiday."

It was one of the rare occasions when O'Callaghan's face betrayed surprise.

"*Me!*" he repeated. "Why?"

"Because Van knows that the bag was in your possession, Patrick. I'm sorry, but that's the way it is. And don't take it out on Kirstie. These people, Van, whoever, they may well think that you peeked inside that envelope. And they'll be right. We all took a look."

O'Callaghan's face paled. "You shouldn't have involved me, John. I don't *need* this sort of stuff."

"What are we doing here?" Raven snapped. "Apportioning blame? You keep banging on about how long we've known one another, how you're the one who always has to bail me out of trouble. Maybe I ought to remind you that it hasn't been a one-sided friendship."

The lawyer moved a pile of mail and looked at the place where it had been.

"You're right, and I'm sorry," he said quietly.

"I've been making some enquiries," said Raven. "I can't find anyone who has heard the name 'Henry Hobart.' "

"Including me," said the lawyer promptly. "Who is he?"

"Cameron's partner. The man who was shot."

O'Callaghan tapped his cigar into the ashtray. "I didn't think the police had released his name."

"They haven't," said Raven. "Cameron told me. Do you realize he doesn't even know who sent them into Hans Security. He just listened to this horseshit that Hobart laid on him and believed every word of it."

"What about the man he's with now, this Van or whoever. He could have set it up."

"Well exactly," said Raven. "That's why I've got to get hold of Sheffield. You'll have to introduce me to him."

"I can't do that," said the lawyer. "I only met the man once. I don't suppose we exchanged more than a dozen words. Lucy Sale thinks he's wonderful, but then she's fascinated by that class of person. You want to meet him, you'll have to do it yourself. He's in the phone book."

Raven reached for his trenchcoat. "Last night you told me to get rid of that bag."

The lawyer tipped the dog from the chair. It grunted resentfully. "I said *you*, not me," said the lawyer hastily. "I can't afford to have anything more to do with it."

Raven brushed some specks from his coat and reached into his pocket. He opened his hand, revealing the plastic card in his palm.

"This just might be of interest to Sheffield."

O'Callaghan leaned over his desk. "What is it?"

"It's what they used to get into the Vaults. And don't ask me where I got it. That's another of those things you're better off not knowing. I'll talk to you soon."

He made his way down to the street and waited for a cab in front of the Portman Hotel. A driver stopped. As Raven climbed into the back of the cab he noticed a motor-cyclist straddling his machine against the kerb. The rider was wearing the full biker's uniform, a helmet with goggles, black leather jacket and thighboots over jeans.

Raven leaned forward and spoke to the driver. "Chelsea Embankment. Go through the park."

The cab headed west on Upper Berkeley Street and entered the park from Bayswater Road. Raven was watching the rearview mirror.

The biker appeared as the cab crossed the bridge over the Serpentine. He followed as far as the Embankment and then wheeled off towards Battersea Bridge. Raven glanced across at Lauterbach's cul-de-sac. Kirstie was still at work. The Ford wasn't there. The lamps were on along the length of the Embankment. The river ran dark on the ebbing tide. Raven descended the steps and opened the door to the gangway. Phosphorescent paint glimmered on the lifebelt. He walked halfway along the deck before he realized that something was wrong. He had left the curtains closed. Now they were open. He tiptoed as far as the door to the sitting room and put an ear to the crack. All he heard was the familiar grinding of chains and the noise of shifting timbers. He opened the door and stepped forward into a scene of total confusion. His desk drawers had been emptied onto the sitting room floor. The cupboards at the end of the room were open. Books, records, photographs were strewn at random. He ran to the kitchen and dragged back the freezer. He dropped through the trapdoor without using the ladder. A naked bulb swung on a length of flex, lighting the junk that was stored below. He yanked up the second hatch. The bag was still in place. He carried it up to the kitchen and wrestled the freezer back across the floor.

He drew a glass of water and wiped his forehead. The closets in the bedroom had been ransacked, clothes strewn across the bed. Photograph frames had been placed facedown, Kirstie's scent bottles shifted from the dresser to the window-ledge. It was the same in the bathroom. The contents of the medicine chest had been emptied into the tub, the laundry basket upturned. A cigarette-end floated in the lavatory bowl. Nothing had been touched in the guestroom. As far as Raven could see, nothing had been stolen. Kirstie's jewel-box was intact. The intruder had left their passports and marriage certificates on top of the desk. Raven lit a smoke and sat down on the couch to assess the damage. The burglary was the work of someone with access to the right sort of equipment. Four high-quality locks had been dealt with. It seemed as though someone was trying to make a point, a practical joke or an act of petty revenge. Like the man on the motor-cycle, the burglar had been contemptuous of discovery.

Raven emptied Cameron's bag into one of Kirstie's camera satchels and set about restoring some sort of order. The first thing to do was to get Kirstie off the boat. He heard the door bang at the end of the gangway. Lauterbach was back after walking the dog. Raven collected the camera-satchel and walked to the neighboring boat. Light streamed from the wheelhouse. The Great Dane turned his head slowly as Raven appeared, the animal's tail semaphoring recognition.

Hank Lauterbach was smoking one of his ultra-thin joints, eyes glinting behind his granny-glasses. He was wearing thick serge trousers and a reefer jacket with brass buttons. His beard was dyed an unnatural shade of black. He looked Raven up and down.

"You'd better watch it, creeping around like that. The dog'll have your ass one of these days."

The American was convinced that the Great Dane was a killer. He offered the joint to Raven.

Raven declined. "What time did you open the shop today?"

Lauterbach rolled his eyes at the wall. "I've no idea. It could have been noon. There's not a lot going down this time of the year." He flicked the roach through the open doorway and watched it spiral away into the darkness. "Why do you ask?"

"Never mind that," Raven said, narrowing his nostrils. "What is that unearthly stink?"

"Unearthly stink?" Lauterbach repeated as though not understanding. "That's the dog's dinner. A sheepshead, her favorite."

The smell came from the galley below. Raven used the door like a fan.

"Were you in the shop all afternoon?"

"Sure was," said Lauterbach. "Right up until we went out for our walk. What is this anyway, some kind of inquisition?"

"I just wondered if you noticed anything out of the ordinary," said Raven. "Anyone suspicious hanging around."

"Not a thing," the American said. He took a keen interest in Raven's activities and longed to be part of them.

Raven stepped out on deck and peered over the side. A rowboat drifted on a line attached to a stanchion.

"I need to borrow your dinghy," he said over his shoulder.

"What do you want it for?" Lauterbach was staring at the satchel Raven was carrying.

"Never mind about that," Raven said. "Just give me the oars."

He climbed down the ropeladder. Rainwater slopped in the bottom of the dinghy. He kept his balance, standing up, as Lauterbach lowered the oars. Raven cast off and began rowing upstream against the current. He stayed close to the periphery of the boats, out of sight from the shore. He held his course for a couple of hundred yards before pulling in to steps cut in the granite blocks. He attached the painter to a ring in the wall and clambered up to the Embankment. The satchel was under his arm. Traffic was heavy but the pavements were empty. Anyone watching his boat would be wasting their time. It was two hundred yards away. He made his way through back streets to Fulham Road, making sure that no-one was following him. He walked into the Miranda Health Club. The girl at the reception desk looked up and smiled. "Mrs. Raven's not in, I'm afraid."

"I know that," he said, showing her the satchel. "I need to leave this in her locker. May I have the key?"

She passed it across the counter. Men and women were passing through on their way to the pool or gymnasium. Clearskinned and brighteyed, they carried themselves with the superior mien of those who take care of their bodies. Raven had no ambitions in that direction. His Sunday jog in the park was enough. The locker-room was at the far end of the building. He deposited the satchel in his wife's locker and returned the key to the girl at Reception. Once outside, he turned up his collar and hurried back to the Embankment. He lowered himself into the dinghy again, his hand sliding down the wall as he sought to maintain a precarious balance. The tide helped his return. The lights were out in the wheelhouse of Lauterbach's boat. No-one responded to Raven's shout. He hauled himself up on deck, leaving the oars in the dinghy.

Kirstie was waiting for him in the sitting room, stretched out on a couch, a Campari-and-soda on the floor at her side. She aimed the zapper at the television set, killing the image as Raven came into the room.

"Where on earth have you been?" she enquired, looking him up and down.

He fixed himself a drink, talking with his back to her. "I had a visitor this morning."

She pushed herself up into a sitting position. "What were you doing in Lauterbach's rowboat? I saw you from the steps."

He carried his glass across and sat down beside her. "I had to put something in your locker at the health club. I didn't want to be seen leaving the boat."

The color of her sweater matched her eyes, he thought.

"In my locker?" she said. "What sort of something?"

He swirled the drink in his glass. "That stuff from the Vaults. It's in one of your satchels."

The news seemed to galvanize her. "Are you out of your mind or what! What am I supposed to say if somebody finds it?"

"It won't *be* found," he said. "It'll be gone long before you go to the health club again." He looked at her and smiled. "I said I had a visitor while you were at the studio—someone from the Department of Immigration. He wanted to talk to Kirk."

She closed her eyes briefly. "O my God!"

"He asked where Kirk was," Raven went on. "I told him, as far as we knew, Kirk had gone back to Paris. The thing is, I don't think he *was* from the Immigration Service. I'm pretty sure he was Special Branch."

The news only increased her anxiety. "I feel terrible. The whole thing is my fault."

"I spoke to Maggie earlier on. I want you to stay with her for a couple of days. She says she'll be glad of your company. Kirk gave your name and address when he arrived at Heathrow. The guy who came here claims there's no record of Kirk leaving the country. They're playing games with us, Kirstie, and I'm not sure why."

She rose with one graceful movement, shaking her head. "I really believed we'd got rid of all that stuff."

"All we have to do is stay cool," he replied. "I'm going to try to get hold of Sheffield, the man whose box Cameron robbed."

"What about the man I saw?" she demanded.

"I don't trust him," said Raven.

"Poor Kirk," she said, close to tears. "I wish I knew where he was."

He grabbed both her wrists, forcing her to look up at him. "Listen to me. We're doing all we can. The way to help him is to help me. Stay with Maggie for a couple of days, go about your business in the usual way. Anyone calls you at the studio you tell the same story as I'm doing. Kirk left the boat yesterday morning. As far as we know he was on his way back to Paris."

"But they'll *know* that's not true," she objected.

"But *we're* not supposed to know," he replied.

"What's happening to us?" Her face was miserable.

He let her wrists go, kissed her lips. Her mouth tasted of mint. *"Nothing's* happening to us," he insisted. "We're a well-adjusted, delightful couple."

She managed a smile. "There are times when I really do love you."

"I'm a lovable fellow," he said. "Kirk's safe where he is for the next thirty-six hours. That should be enough time for me to make other arrangements. I'm going to try to get hold of Sheffield to-night."

She put on her back-to-the-wall side of her character. "I'll need a toothbrush and things if I'm going to Maggie's."

She came back from the bedroom carrying an overnight bag with a fleur-de-lys woven into the material. She pulled on her Burberry and adjusted her beret in front of the mirror.

"Ok, I'm ready."

They sat in the Fiesta, buckling their seatbelts. Raven moved the car to the end of the cul-de-sac. Kirstie followed the direction of her husband's stare.

"What is it?" she whispered.

A single headlamp swept the pub forecourt.

"The biker," he said. "He was on my tail earlier. Pay him no heed."

"But he'll know where we're going."

"I said don't worry about it, Kirstie. And don't call the boat. Jerry said that our phone's tapped."

"It really doesn't change, does it," she said, her eyes still fixed on the pub forecourt. The single light shone through the trees. He pulled the card-key from his pocket and showed it to her. "Don't worry about it, this is my ace in the hole."

She leaned back against the headrest and shut her eyes. Raven turned left into the eastbound traffic. The biker wheeled out after them. He stayed there, traveling twenty yards behind. He vanished when Raven turned into Hollywood Mews. Maggie Sanchez's house had a pink stucco front and a Venetian lamp hanging over the entrance. The street door opened before Raven had stopped the engine. Maggie Sanchez peered out short-sightedly, her glossy black hair hanging straight to her shoulders. She was six feet two inches tall with the bone structure of her Mayan grandmother. She wore a man's flannel shirt over pegtop trousers and sandals with thongs. She bustled them into the hallway and stood with her back against the door. Mexican masks and blankets blazed on the walls. Raven knew the house well. Maggie's murdered lover had been his friend. Maggie took Kirstie's bag and pointed up the stairs. "You room's ready," she said, and turned to Raven. "How long have I got her for?"

"Two or three days." He placed an arm around his wife and drew her close. "Get a good night's rest and don't worry," he said. "I'll call you later."

He kissed Maggie's cheek and let himself out. Water gurgled in the guttering overhead. Rain deadened the sound of his footsteps as he ran to the end of the mews. The biker was waiting for him in Priory Walk, straddling his machine and smoking a cigarette. He was still wearing his goggles. The glow from his smoke lit his features as he inhaled.

"You're beginning to get on my nerves," Raven said. "Who the hell do you think you are?"

The biker moved very deliberately, dropping his cigarette to the ground and stomping on it with the heel of his heavy boot.

"What did you say?" The voice went with the rest of him.

"Sod off!" Raven answered.

The biker removed a gauntlet and scratched the back of his ear. His jacket glistened in the rain.

"You better watch your language," he warned.

Raven circled the machine, noting the details on the registration disk. The bike was a collapsible Honda. Front wheels and handlebars folded back, decreasing the length by half. The Honda would fit in the trunk of a car.

Raven came to a halt in front of the rider. "I don't know what your game is, friend, but be very sure of one thing. You keep following me and I'll have you under a bus. Do I make myself clear?"

The biker notched up his goggles, revealing hostile eyes. "You won't do shit," he said with contempt. "You're a has-been." He continued to stare for fully a minute then pulled down his goggles and trod on the kick-start. He roared out of Priory Walk and turned the corner.

Raven walked back to the Fiesta. Maggie Sanchez's house was ablaze with lights. He drove as far as the pay-phones on Fulham Road. A man's voice replied to his call.

"Mister Paul Sheffield?" asked Raven.

"Speaking." The voice was cultured.

"My name's John Raven. I think we should meet."

Sheffield's tone was relaxed. "Where are you now, Mister Raven?"

"I'm in Fulham, but I'm mobile."

"Then you'd better come to my home," Sheffield said. "I take it you know where I live?"

"I'll be there in half-an-hour," Raven promised.

"Alone, of course." The smile sounded through words.

"Alone," Raven promised.

The white-fronted Edwardian house stood on the rise leading up to Holland Park. There were three plane trees in a small paved yard. A stone eagle glared from a niche above the front door. The windows were shuttered. Raven pressed the bell-push. The front door clicked open immediately. The hallway was as quiet as a church at midnight, the parquet floor strewn with oriental rugs. Flowers were tastefully arranged in a vase on the marble-topped table.

The man who opened the door of the flat was smiling. He was solidly built and dressed in a grey herringbone suit worn with a black silk tie and black brogues. His brown hair was neatly trimmed and his right eye was made of glass. The iris was black. That of his live eye was blue. The combined effect was disconcerting.

Sheffield held out his hand. "Let me take your coat," he invited.

Raven passed his trenchcoat to the other man and watched disbelievingly as Sheffield draped the coat on a hanger and went through the pockets.

"I'm sorry about this," Sheffield said amiably. "Have you any objection to being searched?"

"You're serious?" Raven said.

Sheffield lifted his hands, still smiling.

Raven placed his hands flat, facing the wall, his legs straddled. Sheffield's technique was practised and deft. He used both hands, feeling down Raven's body and limbs. He dipped into pockets without removing the contents and paid special attention to Raven's midriff and the small of his back.

Sheffield touched Raven's shoulder. "Thank you," he said politely. "Come on through."

The adjoining room was at the front of the house and had a high scalloped ceiling. Gas-logs burned in the fireplace. The long sofa was upholstered in soft blue tweed. There were good chairs and a Georgian writing-desk. The pale grey walls were hung with seascapes. A silver-framed photograph on the writing-desk portrayed a group of men about to board a Lysander troop-carrier. All four were wearing camouflage uniforms. Sheffield stood in the forefront.

Sheffield waved him to a couch. "Sit down," he invited. "What can I get you to drink?"

He opened a brassbound chest. Lights came on inside, displaying an array of bottles.

"Scotch-and-water, no ice, please." Raven lowered himself onto the couch.

Sheffield poured three fingers of scotch into a Waterford tumbler and added Spa water. He fixed himself the same and carried both glasses across. The couch sank under his weight as he sat down next to Raven.

"You know who I am," he said, raising his glass.

Raven nodded. "Cyclops Security."

Sheffield leaned back comfortably. "I must apologise for the performance just now. I'm paranoid about people being wired. Apart from the lady living downstairs, we're alone in the house."

Raven could see through a half-open door into what was clearly a bedroom. A rowing machine stood on the floor in front of the dressing-table.

"Alone," Sheffield repeated. "What can I do for you?"

Raven relinquished his glass. "Over the past few hours I've been visited by somebody claiming to be from the Immigration Service. My home has been burgled and I've been followed by a thug on a motor-cycle. On top of all that, my phone has been bugged."

Sheffield showed no surprise. "Suppose we get something straight here," he said. "These things you say have been happening, you think I've got something to do with it?"

"You or the people you work for," Raven said steadily.

Sheffield's live eye roved to his drink. He took a measured sip from it.

"We'll let that pass for the moment. Let's talk about you, Mister Raven. You've been described to me as a man whose sole purpose since leaving the police force has been to destroy it. Clearly an exaggeration. In somebody else's opinion you're a man with delusions of grandeur. I've had as much said about me." His smile was back.

"I've got a lot of critics," said Raven. He found the pack of Gitanes and lit one. "The reason I'm here is this. Some property that I think could be yours has come into my possession, inadvertently, let me add."

"That much I already knew," Sheffield said. His voice and manner remained friendly. "Before we go any further, let me tell you something about myself. I went straight from school to Sandhurst. I had a rough time as a cadet but I managed to get a posting to the Brigade. Three years of that and 18 SAS took me on. I learned about killing and I learned about comradeship. I thought what I was doing was right. I still do."

Raven shifted his legs. Runaway conversations disconcerted him. He liked to retain a firm grip on the reins.

"If you're about to harangue me on the virtue of patriotism," he said, "save your breath. I carry the same passport as you do but when I look around I don't like much of what I see."

"You wouldn't," said Sheffield. "Any more than I do. A teenager with an Armalite knocked this eye out in Northern Ireland. My mates managed to get me clear before the little bastard could squeeze off a second round. They dragged me into an alley that stank of piss and stayed with me until the ambulance arrived. If it hadn't been for them I'd be dead."

Sheffield picked up his glass again. "When I started Cyclops Security, I decided I'd only employ men from the regiment. Everyone joined on the same basis, the concept of loyalty, one to another. There are no ranks, badges or uniforms. Nothing but the certainty that the back you protect is your own. That concept made Cyclops the best of its kind in the country."

Raven flicked ash at the container. "I don't wish to sound insulting, but the truth is I don't give a fiddler's about what makes you so special. I'm concerned that because of you my wife can't sleep in her own bed. She doesn't like that, nor do I."

Sheffield leaned back, hands locked behind his head. "In the first place, you're wrong in your premise that I'm responsible. Now I'm going to say something against my better judgement."

Raven found himself smiling. "I doubt that you've ever done that in your life." It occurred to him that he had had nothing to eat since breakfast. The drink had gone straight to his head.

"Bear with me," Sheffield said sharply. "Ok, we both know that somebody broke into my safety-deposit box. A number of confidential documents were removed."

Raven's yawn was involuntary. "Since we're supposed to be talking frankly," he said, "the whole problem's aggravated by the fact that—I don't know, we seem to start off on opposite sides. The truth is, I suppose, I don't much care for the sort of work you do. All those little jobs that other people are too scared to handle."

"Like what?" Sheffield demanded.

"Murder," said Raven.

In that moment Sheffield's face was as deadly as a crocodile hunting.

"What the hell do you know about what we do?" he asked quietly.

"I keep my ears open," said Raven. "And I'll tell you something else. You want to know why nobody bangs on your door? You work with the Blessing, that's why. You do their dirty work, they protect your ass. That little episode must have had your friends reaching for the smelling salts. I can only guess what's behind it all but I'm sure about one thing. If the press ever gets hold of the truth, the people behind you are going to disown you. And when that happens, goodbye Cyclops Security."

Sheffield's expression showed no change. "Think about your own position," he urged. "You and your wife are locked in tight to the robbery. Cameron stayed on your boat. Your wife was at school with him. The only man who could help prove your story is dead. I'm assuming that you already know how the police feel about you."

"I know," Raven said. "It's a feeling that's mutual."

Sheffield swiveled his good eye. "All those old-timers at the Yard, the ones who remember you, they're just waiting to shaft you, for once and for all. So when you look at it sensibly, you and I *are* on the same side, like it or not. On the basis of my enemy's enemy is my friend."

Raven looked at the other man, gauging his strength. "So what is your proposition?"

"Return my property and I'll take care of everything else. I'll get Cameron out of the country. You and your wife can take a holiday. Come back and everything will be normal again."

"That's weird," Raven said. "I've had exactly the same offer from somebody else. Someone who claims that the stuff in the locker belongs to him."

Sheffield leaned forward, anticipating every word that came out of Raven's mouth. "Who?"

"The guy who's got hold of Cameron. I've only spoken to him on the phone. My wife's actually seen him."

"Did she describe him?"

Raven shrugged. "She said he was evil." He produced the card from his pocket and placed it on the table between them. "Do you recognize this?"

Sheffield held the card by its edges. "Yes."

"I take it that every customer has one of these so we know that the man *is* a customer. He won't have given his right name, of course," Raven said.

Sheffield scratched an eyebrow. "I doubt that anyone does. My box was the only one broken into."

"There's something else," Raven continued. "I've got the surveillance tapes from the Vaults. They could be useful. You can keep the card."

Sheffield put it away in his wallet. "Do we know this other man's name?"

"Van," Raven answered. "That's all we've got up to now. That and a telephone number. Cameron seems to live in a different world. He claims that he thought he was helping some woman. He was conned from the start. Some tale about working for a solicitor, a woman with heavy domestic problems."

"You've no idea how Van got hold of him?" Sheffield asked.

"None," said Raven. "Cameron just walked off the boat. I wasn't there. Next thing that happened was that my wife got this phone call."

Sheffield leaned forward again. "Are you willing to trust me?"

Raven thought for a couple of seconds. "It's a matter of expediency rather than trust," he decided. "That's why I've come to you. I want my life to be the same as it was a few days ago. If you can make that happen, then you're my man."

Sheffield listened intently as Raven explained what he had in mind.

"It could work," Sheffield said when Raven was done.

"And you think you can get the sort of help we need?"

Sheffield nodded. "I'm not sure for how long."

Raven lifted the handset and dialled. Van Hall's voice replied.

Raven leaned into the mouthpiece, his voice low and urgent. "I can't talk on the phone but I have to see you. Something's come up. Where can we meet?"

There was a long pause before van Hall answered. "Where did you have in mind?"

"Anywhere you say."

Sheffield was whistling softly. Raven made a silencing motion with his hand.

"Do you know Haddon's on Old Brompton Road?"

"Opposite the bank," Raven said quickly.

"I'll be there in half-an-hour," van Hall promised.

Raven frowned. "How will we know one another?"

"Don't worry about that," said van Hall. "I'll know you."

Raven cradled the phone and looked up. "Did you get all that?"

Sheffield was on his feet, turning out the bedroom lights. "I heard. We'll be round the corner, outside the Onslow Hotel. A blue Range Rover, Y registration. Is there anything you need?"

Raven tightened the belt on his trenchcoat. "Luck," he said soberly.

Raven pulled the Ford in behind the Lycée and walked around the corner. Haddon's Bar & Gallery was opposite. Lights shone through rainstreaked windows onto the shining pavements. There were no individual tables, just counters and stools. Filipino waitresses dealt drinks and fast-food. It was a bar where students hung out, noisy and cheerful. Musak played non-stop. The weather had taken its toll. The large room was half-empty. Raven sat on a stool facing the plateglass window. He ordered coffee and scrambled eggs and ate with one eye on the entrance. It was difficult to see who came in or went out. People were crowding round the cashier's desk, blocking the way. Raven finished his meal and lit a cigarette. At twenty minutes past eight a man eased himself onto the stool next to Raven. Raven continued to stare straight ahead. The newcomer's reflection showed in the window.

"Good evening!"

Raven recognized the voice and turned his head. The man was in his early forties with thinning brown hair and a suntan. He was expensively dressed with a velvet collar turned up on his dark blue vicuna overcoat. He leveled the unwinking stare of a cobra.

"What is the problem?"

A waitress brought van Hall's coffee. Raven waited until she had gone before answering. "It's my lawyer. I already told you, there was a death in his family. He's taking care of the funeral arrangements. That means that he won't be back until Thursday!"

Van Hall cradled his cup in both hands. His nose thinned as he sniffed the coffee. He put it down untasted.

"I think you're lying," he said.

Raven flicked ash at the saucer. "Then you're not as smart as I thought you were. Why should I lie?"

"That's what I'm wondering."

The cigarette bobbed in Raven's lips. "I'm the one who's taking the risks. I'm not even sure that Cameron's still with you."

Van Hall scanned the length of wet street and opened umbrellas.

"You can rest assured that he's dry and comfortable."

Raven reached for both bills. "I seem to be wasting my time."

"Tell me what's on your mind," said van Hall.

"It's the same as before. Cameron gets transport, you get the goods. The only thing that's changed is the date of delivery. And there's nothing I can do about that."

Van Hall picked up his gloves. "What's your lawyer's name?"

"I've told you all you need to know," Raven said. "Take it or leave it."

Van Hall leaked a smile. "I want one thing clearly understood. Either you deliver on Thursday or your friend's on the street."

"I'll keep my end of the bargain," said Raven.

"You better had," said van Hall. "Be at the Cadogan Hotel at two o'clock on Thursday afternoon. The hall porter will have an envelope for you. I'll tell you where to meet me."

"Two o'clock is too early," said Raven. "I won't have the bag by then."

"Just be there at two," said van Hall. "You can do what you have to do later. And by the way, that telephone number I gave you no longer works."

Raven moved his shoulders. "You haven't told me when Cameron will be back in France."

"That's because I don't know," van Hall said, coming to his feet. "Within hours of me making a phone call, that's all I can tell you."

He turned away as though leaving a stranger. Raven watched him as far as the exit. The street swallowed him seconds later. Raven lifted van Hall's coffee cup by the handle. He emptied the liquid into his own cup and placed van Hall's cup in a small plastic bag. He sealed the neck with a snapper-ring and hurried outside. The blue Range Rover was parked as promised, a hundred yards away, in front of the Onslow Hotel. Sheffield opened the rear door. He was sitting next to the driver. He placed the plastic bag in the glove compartment, using the care of a surgeon.

"This is Tomek Iampolski," said Sheffield, indicating the man next to him. "He's a comrade."

The driver had a crop of prematurely white hair and wore a black leather jacket over sweater and jeans. He offered Raven his hand.

"Can I use your phone?" Raven asked.

Sheffield gave him the radio handset. Raven dialed and Maggie Sanchez picked up the instrument.

"Tell Kirstie I'll be round in half-an-hour," Raven said. He replaced the phone in Sheffield's lap. "I'll talk to you later."

The Range Rover dropped Sheffield at the bottom of Carlton House Terrace. He stood at the top of the steps leading down to the Mall. The only car in sight was parked between street lamps, twenty yards away. It showed no lights and was apparently unoccupied.

Sheffield started walking. As he neared the car, a man appeared behind the steering wheel. The passenger door was opened. Sheffield slipped in beside Frazer. It was too dark to see Frazer's expression but his tone was resentful.

"These calls, out of the blue," he complained. "You're putting me under a lot of pressure."

"Not for much longer," said Sheffield. He placed the bag containing the cup on the seat between them. "Be careful with this. Hold it by the neck," he warned. "You should get a good set of prints from it."

Frazer looked down, shaking his head. "I don't know what you're trying to do to me. Someone starts asking questions I'm right in the shit."

Sheffield wriggled back in his seat until his shoulders touched the door.

"Breaking into Raven's boat, putting a tail on him. You never mentioned any of that the last time I saw you."

The interior of the car smelled of the mints Frazer was chewing. "That was down to this nutter in charge of the case. It all stopped as of that day. All of it."

"I'm glad to hear it," said Sheffield. He lodged the plastic bag in the glove compartment. "What are they saying up on the fifth floor?"

"Nothing," said Frazer. "And I'll tell you something else, mention your name and you draw a blank. Nobody wants to know you. Look, I'm thirty-three months away from retirement. Have you thought about that, thought about the risks I'm running?"

Sheffield flapped a reassuring hand. "People *like* you, Joe. They even respect you. Not only that, you've got friends in high places. Plus you're a Mason."

The Special Branch man lowered his window and dragged wet air into his lungs. He seemed to have difficulty in breathing.

"None of that's going to matter, they find you in my car," he said.

Sheffield touched a switch. A soft light came on in the roof. He could see the other man's face. "Now, February seven," he said quietly. "Year before last. You called me, one o'clock in the morning, asking for help. Can you remember what I said?"

A group of people dressed for the evening found their way down the steps and walked past the car. Frazer wound up his window again.

"You mean word for word?"

"I said 'when and where,' " Sheffield said. He offered no quarter. "That girl was close to death. Lying on your bedroom floor totally out of it, with her veins pumped full of smack."

Frazer licked his lips furtively, turning his head away. "I never knew she was into the stuff," he muttered.

"Bullshit!" said Sheffield. "She was twenty-two years old and you were dicking her. You even gave her a key to the place."

"My wife had just left me," Frazer said doggedly.

"Left you because of this other bimbo," said Sheffield. "You were in bad bad trouble. You came to me because there was nobody else you could ask. Nobody else daft enough to drive the woman eighteen miles to the hospital and wait there until they said that she'd live. We saved your ass, Joe. You didn't go to your other friends then for help."

Frazer let his breath go in a long-drawn-out sigh. "I've been waiting for this," he said resignedly.

"Put the harmonica away," Sheffield said. "A man's supposed to pay his debts and I'm calling one in. It's as simple as that!"

A near shriek came from Frazer's throat. "*Simple!*" His expression dissolved in frustration. "It isn't just getting the prints, it's the rest of the shit that goes with it. People are bound to ask questions."

"Like who, for instance?" Sheffield insisted. "You know the right places to go. Use the old grip or whatever it is that you Masons do. Tell the man that it's something that you want kept private. He'll understand. That's all that you have to do. I take care of the rest."

Frazer glanced up from the floor. "If I'd heard this from any-one else, I wouldn't believe it."

"Believe it," said Sheffield. "I've got four women to deal with, each of them looking to me for answers. I sent their men to their deaths. That's more important than your problems or mine, Joe."

Frazer appeared to have shrunk within his clothing. "I wish I'd never laid eyes on the bitch."

"You wanted to help her," Sheffield smiled. "That's what makes the world go round, Joe. Aid and tenderness, one towards the other."

When Frazer spoke again, his resistance had collapsed entirely. "You can be a savage bastard at times."

"A realist," Sheffield corrected. "I can tell you what happened to your little friend if it'll make you feel better."

Frazer's eyes narrowed. "She's not dead, is she?"

"Alive and as well as anyone could be with a habit like hers. One of my guys saw her a couple of months ago in Edinburgh. He drove her to the hospital that night."

Frazer was happy to drop the subject. "I do this for you and I've paid my dues, is that what you're saying?"

Sheffield lowered the lid over his glass eye. "That's exactly what I'm saying, Joe. The next one's on me."

"There won't *be* any next one," Frazer said with feeling. He looked at his watch. "This will take a couple of hours, at least. What are you going to do?"

"I'll be in the Range Rover," Sheffield said. "You've got the mobile phone number. Give me a call when you're through. Drop me off on Trafalgar Square."

Traffic signals held them at Admiralty Arch. Sheffield saw the Range Rover, waiting outside the National Gallery. His voice was casual. "Have there been any sightings of Cameron?"

Frazer turned his head sideways. "I'm doing what you asked me to do, right?"

"You're doing fine," Sheffield said.

Frazer put the car in gear and let in the clutch. "Then please don't play games with me."

The car stopped and Sheffield transferred to the Range Rover. He smiled at the driver.

"On time as usual."

"And I can poach eggs," said the Pole. "You want to make me an offer?"

"We'll sit in the park for a while," Sheffield said. The Range Rover moved back around the square.

Tomek Iampolski was the son of a Polish World War 2 fighter pilot and a Nottingham barmaid. He had chosen the army in preference to reform school and had been Sheffield's right-hand man for the last two years. He bulled the Range Rover into the freeforall at Hyde Park Corner. Once into the park, he pulled to a halt. Bareboned trees dripped like leaking cisterns on both sides of the peripheral avenue. Beyond the blurred lamplight the wet darkness stretched into the distance. The occasional car sped past, spraying slush. Nothing stopped. Iampolski cut the headlamps and leaned forward, drumming his fingers on the steering wheel.

"Is Frazer giving us trouble?" he asked.

"Not really," said Sheffield. "He just needs the odd yank on the chain." He had no secrets from the other man. It was the Pole who had driven Katie Hoyt to the hospital. Sheffield trusted his judgement. "What do you think of Raven?" Sheffield asked suddenly.

Iampolski terminated his finger-drumming. "In what way?"

Sheffield offered his cigarettes. "Would you trust him?"

The Pole blew twin streams of smoke through thinned nostrils. "It ain't in my nature to trust people, Paul. Except for you and the others, I don't trust nobody."

Sheffield understood all too well. The comradeship of army life engendered contempt for civilians. The four men killed in Chile had been part of the only family that Iampolski had ever known. Their deaths had left him bewildered and angry.

"Do you think he's a liar?" Sheffield persisted.

The cigarette glowed under Iampolski's nose. "I don't know the geezer, but I don't think so, no. He ain't got much reason to lie."

"That's what I'm talking about," Sheffield said. "I like the way he thinks."

"He was a copper, wasn't he?" The way the Pole said it was a denouncement.

"He's a rebel, like you and like me," Sheffield said. "What's the matter, Tomek, don't you like what we're doing?"

Iampolski smiled bleakly. "I wouldn't be here if I didn't. I lost four good mates, people I fought with, got pissed with. I feel the same way about them as you do."

"What we're doing is Raven's idea," Sheffield said. "For the time being he's one of us, Tomek. If this thing works, it'll be thanks to him."

"And if it don't?"

Sheffield found himself smiling. "Then you and I are going to be looking for another job." He shivered and closed the window. "Let's get the hell out of here, it's beginning to depress me."

Iampolski turned the ignition key. Motor and lights came alive.

"You're the boss," he said quietly.

TWELVE

The XJ6 came to a halt. Van Hall let himself into the lobby. There was no sound at all from inside the flat. He inserted the key in the lock and pushed the door open. A light came on in the kitchen. Cameron was standing behind the ironing-board in his shirt and shorts. He was pressing his jacket and trousers.

"I heard the car," he said.

"Get your clothes on," said van Hall. "We're moving."

He glanced round the flat as Cameron dressed. He had paid the agency a month's rent in advance, giving a false name. Cameron came into the sitting room, his red hair sleek with water.

"What's the name of Raven's lawyer?" van Hall demanded.

The Canadian shrugged and reached for a cigarette. "I don't know."

"How do you mean, you don't know?" said van Hall. "You met him on the boat. You must know his name."

"I didn't hear it," Cameron argued.

"You mean they talked in sign-language?" Van Hall's tone was sarcastic.

Cameron held up a hand. "Back off, for God's sake. You're making me nervous. If you'll give me a chance, I'll tell you what happened. In the first place, I'd just seen someone's head blown off. Remember that. It was no time for polite conversation. If the lawyer's name was mentioned, I never heard it."

"Which of them took the bag?"

"I don't know that either," the Canadian said. "All I know is that somebody had it when they left the boat. I wasn't there when Raven came back."

"Raven claims he can't get the bag until Thursday."

"If that's what he says, then it's true," Cameron said.

"You'd better hope so," van Hall answered. "Let's go."

Van Hall parked the Jaguar on Kinnerton Street, forty yards away from the house. Cameron followed him into the hallway. Van Hall picked up the mail and nodded across at the kitchen.

"Fix yourself something to eat if you're hungry." Cameron was looking around the place appraisingly. "Don't touch the phones and keep away from the windows," warned van Hall.

Cameron moved his head in assent. The two men climbed the stairs. Van Hall opened the door leading to the guestroom. The furniture was pine, the fabric furnishings Laura Ashley. Victoria sporting prints hung on the walls. Van Hall closed the curtains.

Cameron bounced on the side of the bed and peeked into a couple of drawers. The move from the Regent's Park flat appeared to have restored his ebullience.

"Not bad," he said cheerfully. "How long am I going to be here?"

Van Hall spoke from the bathroom doorway. "A couple of nights." Clean towels hung on the side of the tub. There was soap and disposable razors. The bedside television worked.

"If the phone rings, don't answer," said van Hall. "And if someone comes to the door while I'm out, don't answer either."

Cameron sat on the side of the bed, pulling off his chukka boots.

"Everything'll be done by the rules. You're looking at a reformed character."

"Keep it that way," said van Hall. He returned downstairs and closed the door to his study. The one message on his answering machine was from his secretary.

Mister Hannay from Chemical Industries called. He wanted to make sure you were back in the UK.

Van Hall rewound the tape. It was costing him two thousand pounds a month to service his debt to the bank. Interest for the last two months was unpaid and the bank was threatening foreclosure. He sat in his favorite chair, the padding adjusting to his shape. The dice was rolling in his favor again—Hobart was dead, the man upstairs no more than a clown, and Sheffield was no longer a problem.

Van Hall's plan was a simple one. Since the attempt upon Pinochet's life, General Molina had been hailed as his President's savior. Proof of his involvement in the coup would destroy him completely. Four million pounds was a fraction of his resources. Molina had no alternative. Pinochet had a reputation for dealing with his enemies swiftly and efficiently. There were two telephones on van Hall's desk. He picked up one of them. A girl's voice answered expectantly.

"Let me talk to Mister Brady, please," van Hall said.

The girl's voice echoed in the handset. "It's someone for you, Dad!"

"Who is it?" The growl was unwelcoming.

"A friend," said van Hall. "I need a favor."

"I don't do no favors," said the voice. "Who gave you this number?"

"Henry Hobart," said van Hall.

Brady's tone was guarded. "What did you say your name was?"

"Van. Henry said that you'd be able to help me. I'm willing to pay, of course. You want to check with Henry first then, do it. I'll call you back."

There was no way in which Brady would know that Hobart was dead. The name had never been publicized.

"What's your problem?" The dock worker's tone held fresh interest.

"I have this friend," said van Hall. "He's in a jam and needs to get out of the country."

"And Henry told you to come to me?"

"That's right."

"This friend of yours, you mean he's got problems with the law?"

"You could say that," said van Hall. "Nothing heavy, you understand. Business worries. He can't afford to answer too many questions. He just wants to leave quickly."

"A thing like this," Brady said doubtfully. "I mean the dock police are lively at the moment. They ain't so much looking for people who want to get out as them what's trying to get in. But it don't make no difference. This class of business is risky."

"My friend's willing to pay two thousand pounds cash," said van Hall.

Brady hesitated. "I don't know. For one thing he'd have to get past the checkpoint. They keep a sharp eye on the gates. Getting him through would mean somebody else with his hand out."

"Two thousand's his limit," said van Hall. "He has to leave before the week-end."

There was a noise of paper rustling. "I've got the list in front of me," Brady said. "There's a freighter out of Athens docking on Friday, twenty hours, Pier Eleven. She'll be loading heavy machinery and she'll leave on the morning tide."

"Bound for where?" van Hall asked.

"Santander. If that'll suit, I just might be able to help you. When would I see the money?"

"My friend will bring it with him."

"I don't want him coming anywhere near my house," Brady said hastily. "I'll make some enquiries. Call me the same time tomorrow and I should have news for you."

Van Hall relinquished the phone. Upstairs, Cameron was lying on the bed watching television with the sound turned off.

"I just booked your passage home," said van Hall.

THIRTEEN

Sheffield and Raven were in the Holland Park Avenue apartment. It was five minutes after 11 P.M. by the clock over the fireplace. Sheffield was still wearing his grey herringbone suit, Raven his cords and flannel shirt. Rain pattered against the double-glazed windows.

Sheffield adjusted the anglepoise lamp so that its light fell across the top of the table. The last two hours had put the two men on first name terms. The rapport seemed to be based upon a mutual, if guarded, respect.

"Which do you want first?" Sheffield smiled. "The good news or the bad?"

Raven widened his hands. The plan was his and he accepted responsibility. "Whichever," he hedged.

Sheffield leaned forward into the light, the change of position releasing a scent of bay rum.

"They managed to lift three good prints from the cup. The top joint of the right index finger and a couple of thumbprints. He's clean as far as the N.B.I. are concerned."

"Shit!" Raven said feelingly. "I was betting on him having some some sort of record."

The Criminal Records Office had been replaced by the National Bureau of Identification. A new system of high-tech programming located and identified a suspect's prints instantaneously.

"That's the bad news," said Sheffield. "Frazer's friend up on the fifth floor ran a cross-check with the Interpol Room. Take a look at what they came up with." He slid a piece of paper across the surface of the table.

Raven studied the computer printout.

SUBJECT identified as Dirk Roland van Hall (a.k.a. Marcus Patten, Klaus Dieter, Mario Castelli et al). SUBJECT born Rotterdam March 28 1942. Dutch national. SUBJECT known to be in possession of numerous false passports including British, Belgian and Dutch. D&I warrants have been executed in Stockholm, May 1978, October 1980 in Beirut. SUBJECT expelled from Ecuador, December 1984.

Sheffield looked up. "What do they mean, D&I warrants?"

Raven loosened his collar. The room was warm and his shirt was thick.

"It's when one member of Interpol asks another to detain and interrogate a suspect. Interpol's got no power of arrest or adjudication. It's no more than a clearinghouse for information. They get one of these D&I requests, it's up to the host country to deal with it in their own way."

Sheffield frowned. "You're saying that the man got pulled *three times* and just walked?"

"That's what it looks like," said Raven. "Either he knew the right answers or he had local help."

He returned his attention to the printout, reading aloud.

SUBJECT'S last known address in the UK   17 Fordham Drive, Richmond, Surrey.

Sheffield broke in again. "Iampolski's already been there. Van Hall's been gone for three years. I had that number you called checked out. It's a flat in a small block near Regent's Park. It's empty. Tomek talked to one of the neighbors. The woman said it was a rental flat. People come and go all the time. She couldn't remember having seen anyone there recently."

"But they *were* there," said Raven. "They must have moved as soon as he came to see me."

Sheffield held up a hand. "Wait until you hear the rest of it."
The digital printing was bold on the flimsy paper.

SUBJECT suspected of illegal arms dealing, extortion, bribery and
corruption. SUBJECT known to have contacts in France, Brazil, Chile
and Egypt. SUBJECT is fluent in Dutch, English, Spanish and French.
Photograph attached.

The black-and-white print was of the kind taken at airports. It
featured a man with sharp, deepset eyes, wearing a seersucker
suit. He was walking across the tarmac followed by a porter carrying a couple of pieces of luggage. The picture was shot in brilliant sunshine. The two-engine plane in the background bore the
logo of Mexican Airlines.

"A good likeness," said Raven. He exchanged one photograph
for another. The second featured a strong-faced man in his fifties,
with a bald head, wearing a dark rumpled suit. The sign on the
shop front behind him read LIBRERIA INGLES.

"Eduardo Barco," said Sheffield. "Ex-Secretary of the Chilean
Communist party. He's been living in exile ever since Pinochet
came to power. Molina's people tried to kill him in Mexico City
last year."

Raven placed the two photographs side by side and compared
them under the light from the anglepoise lamp.

"Couldn't be better," he said, raising his head. He put the two
photographs and computer printout in an envelope and placed
this in an inside pocket.

"You think your wife can handle it?" Sheffield asked.

Raven pulled himself up. "You'd be surprised at the things that
she *can* handle."

Sheffield lifted a curtain and looked down at the street.

"We don't have much time," he said, turning round to face
Raven.

Raven's smile came and went with the speed of a camera-shut-
ter.

It was the moment both men had been waiting for. "I've got
your stuff down in the car."

Sheffield nodded. "We'll do it tomorrow. I'll give you a name
that'll get you into the embassy." He looked around the room
then opened the door to the hallway. "It'll work," he said with
assurance. "It's the best thing that can happen. The Foreign Of-

fice don't want an arrest. There'll be an inquest on the man who was killed, the proceedings held in camera with no press or public allowed. Then they'll shake hands all round, tell each other 'jolly good show' and that'll be that."

Raven slipped into his trenchcoat. "You're sure that Cameron's going to be allright?"

"Certain," said Sheffield. "These people don't care about you or me and least of all Cameron. What they want is to get rid of him." He closed the front door behind them.

Raven stopped on impulse. "I don't like your line of business," he said.

Sheffield opened the street door. Cold wet air blew in their faces.

"Nobody asked you to. I'm happy for you to be the idealist."

"I'm talking about things that I feel are right or wrong," Raven answered. "To use your own words, you sent four men to their deaths, but you're honoring your commitment to their dependents. In my book that's right. What I'm doing is defending my wife in the best way I can. And that's right, too."

They walked the thirty yards to the Fiesta. Raven opened the trunk and drew out the camera satchel. The two men sat side by side in the Ford. Headlamps came on behind them, laying a hard pattern of light across the shiny blacktop. Raven swung round hurriedly.

"Don't worry," said Sheffield. "It's Tomek, keeping an eye on things."

Raven dropped the satchel in Sheffield's lap. "Check it," he urged.

Sheffield reached down deep and withdrew one of the video cassettes.

"Surveillance tapes," Raven said. "Van Hall's worried about them and the card-key."

Sheffield closed the satchel and returned it. "Anything that keeps him happy. I'll see you at eight-thirty tomorrow morning."

Raven offered his hand. He watched Sheffield as far as the Range Rover before turning the ignition key. He was outside Maggie Sanchez's house twenty minutes later. The street door opened before he could switch off the motor. Kirstie hurried out, her velvet beret pulled low, her Burberry slung round her shoulders. She took the seat beside Raven and inspected him.

"You look absolutely terrible," she said. "You're getting too fragile for this kind of stuff. I worry."

"So do I," he said. "This whole thing's too outrageous, even for me. I'm going to the Chilean Embassy tomorrow morning. Sheffield's got a name that'll get me in."

She frowned, adjusting her seatbelt with nervous fingers. "I don't understand," she said. "Why is Kirk with this man if the police aren't supposed to be looking for him? Why doesn't Kirk just walk away?"

"Because he doesn't know that he's off the hook. Sheffield's the only one who knows what the other side's doing."

"The other side," she said, pinching her mouth in. "You talk as if it was some kind of game, with rules and teams. Why does it have to be you who goes to the embassy?"

Raven let in the clutch. "Because I'm the only one who can do it."

He took a left on Fulham Road and drove north towards Knightsbridge. There was no sign of the man on the motor-cycle. No-one had been near the boat. They drove up Park Lane, then Raven swung right onto Curzon Street. A few hookers loitered in the doorways. Other than that, Shepherd Market was empty. Raven turned the Fiesta into the mews. Kirstie unlocked the outside door to the studio and they climbed the stairs. Kirstie lowered the venetian blinds, took off her beret and shook her hair loose. Raven hung her coat on the stand and placed the two pictures Sheffield had given him side by side on the plastic-topped desk. Kirstie positioned the anglelamp and inspected the glossy prints. Her tone was chirpy and businesslike.

"You want a composite with van Hall standing next to this other man, is that it?"

"Right. It's got to look natural," he emphasised.

She pulled a headband from a drawer and tied it round her hair. "Easy," she said. "A sixteen-year-old trainee could do it."

"I don't know any sixteen-year-old trainees," he replied. He looked at his watch. "How long is this going to take?" he asked anxiously.

"Not long," she said, scanning the lights and the meter. "You can give me a hand with the camera."

He opened the door to the working area. There were no windows. An oblong of green baize was fixed to the white-painted wall. The 5.5 Sinar perched on a monopad. Raven rolled it across the floor so that the lens faced the green baize. Kirstie placed two Bowen lamps, each with a bowl-reflector, one on each side of the camera. She fitted a Polaroid pack to the back of the Sinar and turned on the lamps. The studio filled with brilliant light.

"Sit down and stay still," she commanded.

Raven straddled a chair. She was at her best under pressure, her movements deft and professional.

She wiped the glossy surface of van Hall's photograph, using a camelhair brush and gum-pencilled it to the baize on the wall. She bent over the camera, adjusting the lens until the image was sharp on the screen. She pressed the shutter-release and waited for twenty seconds. She peeled off the Polaroid pack and laid it on the work-bench. She ran a black felt pen around the edges of the Polaroid print and applied it to the picture of the Chilean communist. She stuck the composite on the baize, reloaded the camera and took the third and last picture. That done, she ran the new print through the photocopier and handed the result to her husband.

"That should teach you not to believe what you see."

He shook his head in admiration. The composite print showed van Hall standing next to the Chilean in front of the Librería Inglés. There was no break of contour, no fuzziness of outline, no hint that the print was a fake.

He blew her a kiss. "You are sensational."

She was wearing one of Maggie Sanchez's sweaters, two sizes too big for her. Her face shone from the heat of the lamps. She put the headband back in the drawer and switched off the lights. They walked down to the empty mews. Maggie was still up when they reached the mews, music playing inside the house. Kirstie unlocked the door.

"Do you want to come in for a moment?"

He glanced at his watch. "No. I'll talk to you first thing in the morning. And don't worry."

She placed her arms round his neck and drew his mouth close to hers. She let him go and lifted a warning finger.

"I need you," she warned. "Remember that!"

He waited outside in the car until the light went out in the hallway. It was a few minutes before midnight when he parked in the cul-de-sac. The rising wind brought movement to the surface of the river. He ran down the steps and let himself onto the boat. He was soundly asleep twenty minutes later.

The traveling clock buzzed like a hornet, the sound invading the bedroom. Raven groped blindly until he stifled the noise. It was 7 A.M. He wriggled out of the sheets and sat on the side of the bed, thinking of the role he was going to play during the next few hours. The knowledge that Sheffield was on his side inspired confidence. He made tea, leaving it to brew while he went out on deck. Early morning traffic moved east towards the city along the Embankment. Gulls wheeled high overhead. The wind that had been blowing all night had dried the pavements and buildings. The river had not abated. Lauterbach's dinghy wallowed on the incoming tide race. There was no sign of the American or his dog. Raven emptied the mailbox. Bills, a couple of invitations, a letter for Kirstie from the Director of Cultural Affairs at Canada House. Back in the kitchen, he poured his tea and made buttered toast, eating with his elbows on the table as he leafed through the newspapers. There had been no mention of the Hans Security robbery since Monday. Everything seemed to bear out Sheffield's account of what was happening behind the scenes.

Raven gave thought to the clothes he would wear. He selected his blue chalk-striped suit with a plain white shirt and grey tie. He did the best he could with his hair. The position he had slept in had left a plume standing at the back of his head, giving him the look of an aging and angry rooster. The door buzzer sounded at twenty past eight. He recognized the voice and released the door. Sheffield was wearing tinted glasses and carrying a briefcase. Raven led the way into the kitchen and switched off the percolator.

Sheffield sat down at the table, his nose thinning as he savored the smell of the coffee.

"How did you sleep?" he enquired.

Raven filled two half-pint mugs with coffee, added cream and brown sugar and pushed one of the mugs across the table.

"I slept well. How about you?"

Sheffield dipped his spoon into the mug. "I've given up worrying."

Raven pushed the composite picture in Sheffield's direction.

Sheffield studied it under the light, took it to the window and carried out a second inspection.

"Perfect," he said, looking up. "Your wife's a very clever lady." He opened his briefcase and removed some papers. "Exhibit number one. Van Hall's rap sheet from Interpol. Exhibit number two, the invoice and check."

Sheffield offered a second sheet of paper. A description of the weaponry used by the four dead men. Four Uzuki machineguns, twelve hand grenades, all Israeli. The car they were driving was a green Citroën stolen in the Avenida Vicuna MacKenna neighborhood and fitted with false registration plates. The dead men entered Chile separately, using forged passports, three British and one South African.

Raven perused the details. George Deerfield, born Chelmsford, May 28, 1953, carpenter. Harold Ewart Stokes, born Gwent, November 28, 1956, painter. Michael Pope, born London, August 10, 1952, farmer. Henry Dupree, born Durban, September 6, 1958, soldier.

There was the address of a woman below. Katherine Hazlitt, 39 Heydon Hill, Caverham, Oxon.

"If they ask, it's her that you're interested in," Sheffield said. "She's thirty years old, unmarried with an eighteen-months-old baby. She's Deerfield's girl friend. Apart from what we're giving her, she's getting sixty-three pounds every fortnight from the DHSS. She knows your name."

Raven put the papers in an envelope. "Van Hall gets everything else," Sheffield said. "The photocopy of the check and the invoice, the surveillance tapes and the card they used to get into the vaults. What time are you meeting him?"

Raven told him and glanced at his watch again. It was five past nine.

"We'd better start moving," he said. He put the two mugs in the sink.

Sheffield pushed his chair back. "Tomek's outside. You've got the carphone number. And remember, we'll never be far away."

The news was welcome. Raven picked up the manila envelope. The two men climbed the steps to the street. The Range Rover was parked near the mouth of the cul-de-sac. Sheffield took the seat next to Iampolski. Raven climbed in behind.

Raven took the carphone from Sheffield.

"No Spanish," warned Sheffield. Raven dialed and a man's voice answered.

"Chilean Embassy. Good morning."

Raven took a deep breath. "I'd like to speak to Mister Peralta, please. My name is John Raven."

The man's voice was musical and heavily stressed. "I am not sure that Señor Peralta is available. Can you please inform me the nature of your business?"

"Just say that it is confidential."

"One moment, please." A pause ensued then the man's voice returned. "When did you wish to come to the embassy, please?"

"Now, if that's possible. The matter is urgent."

"One moment, please!" There was another pause before the conversation resumed. "Mister Peralta will see you, sir. Please to give your name when you arrive."

Raven returned the phone to Sheffield. The Pole was chewing a stick of gum.

"You heard that?" Raven asked.

Sheffield nodded and cradled the carphone. "So far so good."

They drove up Marylebone Lane, then right onto Devonshire Street. The Chilean flag hung on a pole outside the entrance to a three-storey white stone building. The Range Rover kept going. A shield above the steps leading down to the basement bore the insignia of the Republic of Chile. A sign said CONSULATE-GENERAL   10 A.M.–2 P.M.

"Drive round the block," Raven instructed.

Sheffield turned in his seat. "There's a garden at the back of the embassy but no back way out. The only exits are through the front door and the basement."

Raven got out of the car and walked back towards Devonshire Street. Most of the houses he passed were clinics or the consulting rooms of medical specialists. It was a hundred and fifty yards back to the embassy. A solid-looking front door barred the way at the top of five steps. On the left of the door a panel was set in the wall. The panel was made of opaque glass the size of a paperback novel. Raven thumbed the bell-push below.

A voice sounded through an unseen speaker. "Yes?"

"John Raven to see Mister Peralta."

"One moment, please."

It was impossible to detect movement behind the frosted glass yet Raven sensed that he was being watched. The street door opened without warning. The man in the hallway was almost as tall as Raven although more solidly built. He was in his mid thirties with the amber eyes and long narrow face of a collie dog. His black hair was well groomed. He was wearing a stylishly cut double-breasted suit and crocodile skin shoes.

"Mister John Raven?" he said, smiling and extending a hand.

A plastic runner protected the floral-patterned carpet. A wide staircase at the end of the hallway climbed past gilt-framed paintings commemorating scenes of colonial conquest. A dark-skinned servant in livery sat at the foot of the staircase.

"I am Pablo Peralta!" The back of the embassy official's fingers were thatched with black silky hairs. "Please come this way," he invited.

They walked up to the second storey. Peralta opened a door and stood to one side.

"Please," he said, waving a hand.

The room they entered had the stiff formality of a museum. The three fifteen-feet-high windows were heavily curtained. The furniture was massive, the walls hung with cut red velvet. Crystal chandeliers reflected the lamps. Peralta waited until Raven was seated.

"How may I help you?" he asked.

Raven took the manila envelope from an inside pocket and placed it on the striped chaise-longue beside him. A faint clatter of office machinery came from below.

"I have to be sure who I am talking to," Raven said.

Peralta smiled again. He leaned back, showing a length of sock as he studied Raven.

"You asked for me by name," he said courteously. "I am First Secretary to his Excellency the Ambassador. You may speak in absolute confidence."

Raven took the fabricated photograph from the envelope and passed it across.

"Do you recognize either of these men, Señor Peralta?"

The First Secretary's inspection was lengthy. He tapped the glossy print with a manicured fingernail.

"One of them is a Chilean national. The other person I do not know. May I ask who gave you my name?"

"You may ask," Raven said, "but I'm not going to tell you. The point is, I'm in possession of the truth about the attempt on General Pinochet's life last September. The coup was organized by the man in charge of the Centro Nacional de Informaciones. General Molina."

Peralta's long face leaked a smile. "Your accent is good. Do you speak Spanish?"

The smile made no impression on Raven. He was watching the flecked tawny eyes. "The second man in the picture is a Dutchman with a number of aliases," Raven said. "His real name is Roland van Hall. Molina hired him to organize the assassination. I take it that you're familiar with the name 'Luis Ortega?' "

Peralta said nothing but the answer was written in his eyes.

"Vanteris SA," Raven elaborated. "Ortega is Molina's godson and paymaster. The sum agreed for van Hall's services was one million pounds. Half of this amount was to be paid up front. When the coup failed, General Molina reneged on the second payment."

Peralta stopped him with an uplifted hand. "Excuse me one moment!"

He shut the door to the hallway as he went out of the room. Raven stayed where he was. The feeling that he was being watched persisted. He glanced round the room for a vantage-point but found nothing. He lit a cigarette and emptied the envelope, making a neat pile of its contents on the table. The door from the landing opened again. Peralta resumed his seat. There was no sign of the photograph he had taken with him.

His voice was languid to the point of indifference.

"You are making a very serious accusation, Mister Raven."

"It's one that can be substantiated," Raven replied. "Here's a copy of Roland van Hall's Interpol record. Take a look at it."

Peralta held the flimsy paper to the light. After a while he selected a cigarette from a lapis-lazuli box. His face was expressionless through the rising cloud of smoke. He offered no comment.

Raven gave him the rest of the documents, identifying each in turn.

"A photocopy of the check signed by Ortega, van Hall's invoice to Vanteris SA. 'For services rendered, five hundred thousand pounds.' You've got the details of the passports used by the four dead men. the car they were driving, the weapons involved. I can understand that you do not like what you see there, Señor Peralta. Betrayal leaves a bitter taste in the throat."

He continued to watch as Peralta studied the documents, referring from one to another as he went. He returned the papers to the manila envelope. "These are photocopies."

Raven widened his stare. "Yes," he agreed.

The diplomat lost none of his urbanity. "Which means that other people have had access to the originals."

"Two," said Raven, holding up fingers. "You're the first Chilean, and that is what counts."

The envelope was close to the Chilean's elbow. "How did you come by this?" he demanded.

Raven smiled. "I used to be a detective at New Scotland Yard. It's easy for you to check that statement. That's all I'm prepared to tell you."

Peralta took another cigarette from the box and rolled it between his fingers, changing its shape from oval to round. He cocked his head. "This address for van Hall in the dossier. Do you know if he's still there?"

Raven moved his head from side to side. "He's long gone. I wouldn't be here if I knew where he was. He's an old friend of Ortega's. They've done business together before. But van Hall's not in Paris. That much I'm sure about."

"And he has no idea that you've come here?"

"None," Raven said. "I'll tell you something else. He's been sighted in London during the past few days."

The diplomat rose, taking the manila envelope to the window. "I must ask you this," he said, turning round. "Why have you come here? What is your interest?"

It was the important question and Raven dealt with it. "The four dead men left dependants, all of them women, one with a child. They're in desperate need and van Hall refuses to help them. I want to make sure that he pays his dues, one way or another. It's as simple as that. Let me be frank. I don't give a damn about your country or your politics. Nor am I in a position to make you do anything. If you can see your way clear to make some sort of contribution to those who have really suffered, then I'll be satisfied. It's a matter for you to decide."

Peralta fingered his silk tie, still watching Raven's expression. Whatever he read there seemed to decide him.

"I shall have to consult my superiors," he said.

Raven rose, brushing ash from his raincoat. "Do whatever you have to. In the meantime, here's my telephone number if you need to get hold of me. There is just one thing. . . ."

Peralta paused at the open door, the manila envelope in his hand.

"I wouldn't want the newspapers to get hold of a story like this," Raven said.

"You have my word," said Peralta. "You will hear from me before the day ends. May I count on your discretion in the meantime?"

"I wouldn't be here if you couldn't," said Raven.

The hallway was quiet, the chair empty at the foot of the stairs. Peralta opened the street door, glanced right and left, then put out his hand.

"I will do what I can for your friends."

The handshake was firm. "Don't sell van Hall short," Raven said. "He'd choke his mother to save his skin. Remember that. It'll stand you in good stead."

The street door closed. The Pole had the Range Rover moving as Raven turned the corner. Raven climbed in behind Sheffield.

"It worked," said Raven. "Goddamit, it worked!" It was difficult to restrain his elation.

Iampolski looked bored. He glanced up at the rearview mirror. "Does someone want to tell me where we're going?"

"Head back towards Chelsea." Sheffield twisted in his seat, looking back at Raven. "What time are you meeting van Hall?"

"Six o'clock, South Kensington Underground Station." Raven shook a Gitane from the pack.

"Open your window," ordered the driver. "Those things stink like a goat's bed."

Raven lowered the window a couple of inches. "He's no fool, Peralta. He just sits there and listens. There's no way you can tell what he thinks."

They crossed onto Marylebone Lane, heading west. "What happened exactly?" asked Sheffield.

Raven went through the discussion as best he remembered. "It must have been a jolt for him. I mean, someone walks in off the street accusing a man like Molina of treason and, what's more, backing it up with hard evidence. Peralta recognized the guy in the picture with van Hall. By the time he read through the Interpol sheet his toes were curling. This was sedition of the very worst kind. Pinochet betrayed by one of his trusted colleagues. Peralta left the room once. I want to bet he was on the phone to Santiago."

They were turning south onto Sloane Street. Sheffield spoke over his shoulder.

"Didn't he ask where you got your information?"

Raven pitched his cigarette at the street. "I said that I'd been a cop. That was all. They could have found that out in any case. He didn't take it any further."

They turned right along the Embankment. Sheffield pointed at the car park in front of the pub.

"Wait for me over there," he told the driver.

Iampolski pulled to the kerb. He rasped phlegm from his throat and spat through the open window.

"What's your part in all this supposed to be?" he enquired.

Peralta's basilisk stare was strong in Raven's memory.

"Vengeance," said Raven. "It's a motive that I'm sure he understands. I told him how van Hall had reneged on the second payment. I told him about the women who'd been left widowed and penniless. I said I wanted nothing for myself. I was in no position to demand one penny from him, I said that if they wanted to make some sort of contribution to the fund for the women, I'd be satisfied."

Iampolski took his eyes away from the rearview mirror. "Them bastards are takers, not givers. Four people, friends of ours, got wasted because of this bloody Pinochet. You think these people are going to lose sleep over the women?"

Sheffield unfastened his door. "You let your brain run too freely," he said to the Pole.

Iampolski voiced Raven's last lingering doubt. "Suppose they start checking the company? I'm thinking about Cyclops."

"It won't get them far," Sheffield answered. "In any case, their concern isn't with Cyclops. They already *know* van Hall is the villain. They've seen his Interpol sheet, a picture of him standing next to someone who spent four years in Moscow."

He lowered himself to the sidewalk and waited for Raven. The Range Rover moved off as the two men descended the steps to the gangway. The deck had been hosed free of bird droppings. Mrs. Burrows had been and gone.

Raven grinned. "You've been here before, I take it?" he said, opening the door to the sitting room.

Sheffield stepped forward, wiping his feet on the mat as he entered the sitting room.

"Not me," he replied, looking round. "That was those clowns from the Branch."

The long room smelled of air-freshener. A note was propped against Kirstie's picture on Raven's desk.

> *She called but didn't leave no message.   Mrs. B.*

"Our cleaning lady," Raven explained. "She doesn't approve of my wife."

He took a couple of bottles of beer from the refrigerator and gave one to Sheffield. They sat facing one another on the two long couches.

"What's on your mind?" Raven asked after a couple of minutes' silence.

Sheffield shrugged, his glass eye catching the light as he moved. "You don't want to take any notice of what Tomek says. He's a good man but he's bitter. Those guys who died were like family to him."

"I'm talking about you, not him," Raven said. "There's something that's bothering you."

"Not really," said Sheffield. He smiled. "I was thinking that maybe you should call your wife."

"It can wait," Raven said. The two men watched as the police launch scythed under the bridge, veered to the Battersea side of the river and continued upstream. "Van Hall's committing suicide," Raven said.

Sheffield lifted his head. His voice was quiet. "Let me tell you about Peralta. He's intelligent, and he's ambitious. What's more, he's a product of the Centro Nacional de Informaciones. He did a year in the school they run for diplomats. The thing is, his allegiance is to Pinochet and not to Molina. I've been thinking, maybe we ought to give van Hall a nudge."

"Like what?" Raven said doubtfully.

Sheffield emptied the beer in his bottle. "I could get someone in Santiago to make an anonymous phone call."

"He wouldn't go for it," Raven said promptly. "In any case we don't have his new number."

"Ok," said Sheffield. "When you see him, tell him you want to be sure he's keeping his side of the bargain."

"That won't be necessary," Raven said. "Know what I think? I think the moment van Hall has his hands on that satchel, he'll call Ortega in Paris. Only by that time Ortega won't *be* there. Peralta will have seen to that. Van Hall's going to put two and two together and he's going to be nervous. If the game's up, anything he's got will be worthless as blackmail. That's when he'll realize that Peralta's his only lifeline. *Trust me,*" he urged. "Now, why don't you have supper with us?"

"I'd like that," Sheffield said, reaching for his hat. A touch of salt blew in as Raven opened the door to the deck.

"We'll see you later, then," Raven said. "Eightish?"

As soon as he heard the door shut at the foot of the steps, he picked up the phone.

It was Kirstie's voice. "Why didn't you call earlier? You said that you would and you knew I'd be anxious."

"I had things to do. I've only just this minute got back on the boat. Look, I want you to knock off early. Go back to Maggie's place and pack your things. You're sleeping with me tonight. The rough stuff is over."

"I can't just walk out like that," she objected. "Maggie's here now as it happens. Shes been keeping me company. Not only that, she has people coming round for supper."

"Then you'll have to make your excuses," he said. "We've got a guest of our own."

He heard the catch in her voice. "You mean *Kirk?*"

"Sheffield," he said. "He's coming to the boat just as soon as I've finished with van Hall. I want you to be there as well."

"There's nothing to eat," she objected. "Except Mrs. Burrows's stodge in the fridge."

"He's not coming for a gourmet experience," he answered. "You can pick up something on your way back."

"What about Kirk?" she demanded. "What's happening to him, for God's sake?"

"Keep your voice down," he warned. "Van Hall's moved him again—I don't know the new number."

"You mean that you're not even sure that he's safe?"

"I'm doing the best that I can," he said. "With any sort of luck, it'll all be over in the next couple of hours. If I'm not back when Sheffield arrives, let him in."

He left the *Albatross* at a quarter to six, carrying the camera satchel. He placed it on the floor next to the driving seat and drove the Fiesta out of the cul-de-sac.

He parked on Harrington Gardens, carried the satchel into the Underground station and waited in front of the florist shop. He had a clear view of the concourse from where he stood. Homebound city workers emerged from the steady stream of trains below, climbing the stairs to the shops in the concourse. Most of them spilled out towards the lights of Old Brompton Road, the foodstores and hairdressers. Students clustered in front of the English language schools. It was the end of the day for most people, the beginning for others.

Raven watched a girl in a man's Raglan coat with upturned sleeves open a violin case. She set up a music-stand in front of her, leaving the violin case open as a receptacle for contributions. A couple of uniformed cops were viewing the scene from nearby. Their expressions showed no more than mild interest.

Van Hall appeared from the north end of the concourse, coat collar turned up, Homburg hat at an angle. He spotted Raven and made his way through the crowd. Raven nodded down at the satchel on the ground.

"It's all there,"

Van Hall leaned over, examining the contents without removing them. He picked up the satchel.

Raven sidestepped smartly, the manoeuvre bringing him directly in front of van Hall, blocking his way to the street. The violinist was playing "Caprice Viennoise."

"We haven't finished our business," Raven said.

Van Hall glanced across at the uniformed policemen. "Maybe you'd like me to ask for help?"

"Why don't you do that?" Raven said, tearing the satchel from van Hall's grasp.

"You're a meddler," said van Hall. "None of this was any of your business."

"I made it my business," Raven answered. "You don't take this satchel until I've spoken to Cameron."

The two cops sauntered towards them. One dropped a coin in the girl's violin case. They walked out to the street.

Van Hall lowered his voice. "He won't answer the phone. I told him to stop away from it."

"We'll try," Raven said, the satchel firmly under his arm. He led the way down the steps to the payphones and herded van Hall into an empty booth.

"Go ahead!" Raven ordered.

He crowded into the booth behind van Hall, committing the number to memory as the Dutchman dialed. He heard the bell ringing at the other end. There was no answer.

Van Hall twisted awkwardly. "We've come too far to screw up now," he said. "Look, there's a boat leaving Southampton in the early hours of tomorrow morning. One last phone call from me and your friend will be on it. I'll get him to call you later. This is his last and only chance."

Raven dropped the satchel at the other man's feet. "See that he makes that call."

By the time Raven reached the top of the steps, van Hall had vanished.

FOURTEEN

Van Hall drove back to Kinnerton Street, sure that he had not been followed. He cradled the satchel in his lap, glancing up the street at his house. The thing to do now was to keep his nerve until the finish. He parked the Jaguar and walked the last few yards to his front door. It was strange. Of the people who could have destroyed his scheme, Hobart had managed to get his head blown off while Sheffield had simply disappeared. Cameron was the only one left.

Van Hall stood in the hallway, listening to the sounds of the house. Music was playing upstairs on the television. The drumbeats reverberated. He removed the envelope and carried the satchel into the kitchen. There were the remains of a meal on the table—rye bread, butter, lemon and an empty package of smoked salmon. The Canadian had found the beer. Van Hall unlocked the door to the patio and upended the surveillance tapes onto the tiles. He doused them with kerosene and struck a match. A burst of flame lit the courtyard walls, held for a while then subsided. A rank smell filled the air. He filled a pail with water and flushed the sludge down the grating. He used the kitchen scissors to chop up the Security Vaults card-key and destroyed the pieces. Other than the documents in the manila envelope, there was nothing

left to link him with the robbery. A letter had been forwarded
from Hans Security, sent to the name and address van Hall had
provided to support his alias. The management of the Vaults informed their customer that a robbery had taken place at the
premises but that the box-holder's property was intact. The management requested the return of all existing card-keys. Replace-
ments would be issued.

Van Hall locked the envelope in his desk and climbed the stairs.
The music was loud inside Cameron's room. Van Hall turned the
door handle. The Canadian was lying on the bed, boots on the
floor beside him. The green corduroy jacket was draped on the
back of a chair. An ashtray filled with cigarette butts stood next
to the boots. Cameron raised himself into a sitting position, his
face wary. Van Hall tossed the Canadian's passport onto the bed.

"You're on your way," said van Hall.

Cameron sunk his head in his hands. It was a moment before he
looked up again.

"You got what you wanted?"

"I usually do," said van Hall. "Now, listen carefully. Get a cab
from here to Waterloo Station and buy a ticket to Southampton
Docks. The journey takes a couple of hours. When you get there,
leave the station by the main exit. You'll see a café right across the
street. Ask at the counter for Joe."

Cameron glanced up, redfaced from the effort of pulling his
boots on.

"What about money?"

"I'll give you money later," said van Hall. "You're lucky you're
not going to be slammed up in some cell sewing mailbags for the
next twenty years."

Cameron inspected his passport before putting it in an inside
pocket.

"Does Raven know about this?" Cameron asked.

"You wouldn't be on your way if he didn't. His phone's still
bugged so we can't call his number. The boat leaves Southampton
in the early hours of the morning. You'll be in Dinard by noon."

He shut the bedroom door and went downstairs to his study.
He removed the two photocopies from the envelope, the canceled
check and the invoice from Cyclops Security. He reached for the
phone. This was the big one. He felt completely in charge. He
knew how much he would ask for. Four million sterling, a sight-

draft drawn on the Swiss Banking Corporation. This kind of money might well put a crimp in General Molina's credit balance but payment would keep him away from the firing-squad. Van Hall had no doubt what Molina would do.

Van Hall composed a Fontainebleau number. A man answered in French.

"Monsieur Ortega," van Hall requested.

"I am sorry, Monsieur. Monsieur Ortega is not available. He is not here."

"Can you tell me when he'll be back?" van Hall asked.

"I regret but I do not know, Monsieur. Monsieur Ortega left for Madrid with Madame and the children two hours ago. I am sorry."

A click terminated the conversation. Van Hall stared at the handset. The servant's voice had been that of a man under stress. Van Hall looked at his watch. It was twenty minutes past nine, twenty past five in Santiago. The Banco de Chile closed at four. Garcia would be at home by now. Electronic signals clicked through to complete the number. Van Hall moved his lips close to the mouthpiece. The phone was lifted at the far end.

"It's me!" said van Hall. The phone was gently replaced. Van Hall dialed again. This time the phone rang without answer.

Van Hall found himself sweating. He wiped his neck with the back of his hand. His body was suddenly chilled. His next call was again to Chile, this time to Viña del Mar. The buzzer sounded three times before a woman picked it up.

"*Dígame!*"

Van Hall spoke in Spanish. "Rolando. What the hell is happening there?"

The whisper was frightened, the stealthy sound of a troubled woman.

"Molina has been arrested. Do not call this number again."

He put the phone down. Anita Cruz was a reporter for *El Diario*. Feared and respected by her competitors, she retained her position by sitting on most of the secrets she uncovered. She had had a working agreement with van Hall for a year. Her news would be up-to-date. Above all, it would be accurate.

Van Hall's hopes exploded around him, leaving the thought of impending bankruptcy. His mind returned to the helter-skelter life of ten years before. The telephone calls at four o'clock in the

morning, the street outside empty except for the one waiting car.
Bile rose in his throat and his stomach churned. He dragged himself up from the chair. Pop music was still pounding away upstairs. Van Hall resumed his place at his desk, aware that his hands were shaking. A resurgence of cunning flooded his brain. Disaster had found him again, striking when least expected. General Molina's position had seemed impregnable. Ortega would never betray his godfather. Filial feeling would be buttressed by self-preservation. Ortega's next destination would be somewhere out-of-reach of the Chilean secret service.

Van Hall looked at himself in the oblong mirror. Raven had seen the telltale documents; so had his lawyer. But what could they mean to them? A cancelled check and an invoice, a couple of names? There'd been no mention of Sheffield in the media. His identity was protected by the people who gave him the license to operate. The pieces clicked into place finally. The informer *had* to be Sheffield. If the British decided that Molina was expendable, then Sheffield would do whatever he was told to do.

Van Hall took a long breath. He still had a hand to play in the poker game. The stakes might be smaller but the pot would still be worth winning. The first thing to do was distance himself from Cameron, get rid of him. He gave the idea fresh thought before going upstairs again. Cameron was fully dressed and sitting in front of the window, with the lights out and the curtains wide open.

Van Hall closed them and switched on the lights. "There's been a change of plan. You're leaving now. Get your things together."

Cameron picked up his mac and checked his pockets for his passport. He looked round the room, pushing fingers through his cropped red hair.

"What about the police?" he said doubtfully.

Van Hall led the way down the stairs. "There hasn't been a word about you in the media since Sunday. All you have to do is keep a low profile. Take a cab to the station, find out which platform your train leaves from and board the train early. No problem. Once you're in the docks, Joe will take care of you. This'll get you to Paris."

He pushed a thousand-franc note into Cameron's hand and opened the door to the street. A light rain was falling outside.

Van Hall stretched out his hand. "Take care of yourself and good luck."

He waited in the doorway until the Canadian had turned the corner, then he closed the door. He picked up the phone in the study.

A voice said, "Chelsea police-station."

"CID," said van Hall.

"DC Beckett speaking."

"The Hans Security Vaults robbery," said van Hall. "You're looking for a man called Kirk Cameron, a Canadian. He's catching the eleven-ten to Southampton Docks from Waterloo Station. He's wearing a plastic mac over a green corduroy suit. He could be armed."

Van Hall punched a couple of digits at random and put the phone down. The manoeuvre prevented the call from being traced. He climbed the stairs, opened the windows in the room that Cameron had used and went into his bathroom. Hot water gushed into the tub. He lowered himself into it gratefully. The tan on his body was fading. He had lived in England too long. It was time for a change of scenery. Tomorrow would give him a new sense of direction.

FIFTEEN

Cameron turned the corner onto Sloane Square. Drifting rain blurred the lamps. He walked south, hugging the wall until a cab cruised by with its light on. The driver stopped and Cameron climbed into the back.

"Waterloo Station," he said, and wedged himself into a corner. The interior smelled of wet plastic. A black-on-white metal sign hung over the two forward seats. THANK YOU FOR NOT SMOKING.

Cameron's position allowed him to see through the rear window without making it obvious. Van Hall's voice echoed in his ears, glib with assurance. The cab turned left along the Embankment, the hiss of tyres on wet hardtop, a background to the sound of the cab radio.

Cameron closed his eyes, memory flooding his mind with sharp images; one dissolving into the next. Henry Hobart in the underground car park, standing for what seemed an eternity, the top of his head hanging in front of his face. Hobart, the private detective turned bank robber. Cameron opened his eyes again. A week ago he had thought that his life had scraped bedrock. His hotel room padlocked, his only hope of a bed a middle-aged harpy who was holding his paintings to ransom. Hobart's lies had changed all that. A couple of chance encounters had altered his life. First

Hobart, then Kirstie. And here he was, a man on the run. He tucked the thousand-franc note inside his passport. The money he had been promised no longer mattered. Setting foot on French soil again was as far as hope took him.

Big Ben was striking ten-thirty as they crossed Westminster Bridge. The driver turned left under the arches, and the cab climbed the long ramp to the terminal. Cameron paid off the driver, and walked into the cavernous railroad station. The concourse was crowded in spite of the lateness of the hour. Passengers were pulling wheeled suitcases. Teenagers struggled with backpacks. Asian women wearing caste marks and saris huddled in family groups. Single-minded pigeons scavenged the filthy floor, avoiding human feet with a streetwise flutter of wings. More pigeons roosted high on the fouled girders, indifferent to the garbled announcements that reverberated under the glass roof. A departure board showed that the next Southampton train would leave from Platform Eight. The train was already in place, its lights not yet turned on. The entrance gates at the end of the platform were closed. A sign read FRONT THREE CARRIAGES FOR SOUTHAMPTON DOCKS.

People waited in front of the gates, surrounded by baggage and plastic containers. Their faces bore the soured resignation of British Rail travelers. There were no benches in sight, no place to sit.

Cameron joined the line waiting in front of the ticket offices. He gained a few places and glanced back at Platform Eight. A ticket inspector was talking to a blind man holding on to the harness of a seeing-eye dog. Lights had come on in the train. The ticket inspector partially opened the gates, allowing the blind man and dog to proceed. The line shuffled forward. The booking-clerk looked up from behind shatterproof glass.

"Where to?"

"Southampton Docks," Cameron said.

The clerk's hand poised above the dispensing machine. "Return or single?"

"Single," said Cameron.

The clerk punched a few keys and placed the ticket in the tray along with Cameron's change. It was ten minutes before eleven o'clock. The entrance gates were still partially open, the ticket inspector standing outside his cubicle. Cameron pushed past the line of waiting passengers and presented his ticket to the inspector. "You want to let me through, please, I'm not feeling too good."

The official was unimpressed. "Gates don't open for another five minutes. You'll have to wait your turn same as everyone else."

Cameron took his place on the end of the line. There were twenty or more people in front of him. Minutes ticked by. The ticket inspector was talking to a hatless man in a raincoat. The man turned his head constantly like a hound that is hunting by sight. A second man was standing on the empty platform, half-concealed by a column supporting a girder. The inspector looked at his watch and threw the gates open. The line surged forward. Cameron turned on his heel and walked away, forcing himself to maintain a saunter. His back felt naked and vulnerable. Most of the station facilities were closed. Only one fast-food bar remained open, its windows directly opposite the entrance to Platform Eight. The man in the raincoat was still scrutinising the passengers boarding the train. His partner was no longer in sight. A British Telecom van was parked on a nearby slip road. The driver turned his head slowly as Cameron veered away, heading for the line of payphones. The Canadian stepped into one and looked back towards the train. People were still boarding.

Cameron dropped a coin and dialed Raven's number. "I'm at Waterloo Station. There are police all over the place."

"Waterloo Station?" Raven's voice was surprised. "What the hell are you doing there?"

"I thought you knew," said Cameron. "I'm supposed to be catching a train to Southampton." Cameron could hear another man's voice in the background.

Raven spoke quietly. "Get out of there fast. Don't go anywhere near the taxis. Use the Underground. Take the first train you see and come straight to the boat. Have you got money?"

"I'm on my way," Cameron said.

Raven replaced the handset. "He's on his way."

They had eaten in the kitchen, salmon steaks that Kirstie had picked up on her way back from the studio and baked in aluminium foil with soya sauce and brown sugar. Raven had provided a bottle of Ayala from the wine racks in the hold. The three of them were in the long sitting room, Kirstie and Raven on the couch nearer the deck, Sheffield opposite. Coffee was percolating

on a spirit lamp. The glass-topped table reflected the flame. Sheffield's face was in shadow. He was wearing a dark grey flannel
suit with a paisley cravat tucked inside his shirt-collar. After a
short bout of initial sparring, Kirstie had clearly taken to him.

She removed the percolator and blew out the light. She filled
the first cup and gave it to Sheffield, addressing her question to
Raven.

"But what is he *doing* at Waterloo Station?"

"Van Hall sent him there," Raven said. "I don't like it. He says
police are all over the place."

Sheffield put his cup down carefully. "Molina was arrested just
after three o'clock this afternoon, our time. The Special Branch
closed the file on Cameron shortly afterwards."

"Is there any way that van Hall could know that?" asked
Raven.

Sheffield moved his head from side to side. "I don't see how. I
got it in strictest confidence. This business about putting Cameron on a boat has to be some sort of set-up."

Kirstie's frown shortened the band of freckles across her nose.
"If Kirk's not in trouble, why are the police at the station?"

Raven shrugged. "We're not sure yet that they are. Kirk may be
imagining things. It wouldn't be surprising after what's happened."

Sheffield shrugged. "Either that or van Hall called some local
police station where the news hasn't filtered through."

"So what happens now?" Kirstie persisted. The black suit she
was wearing displayed her long legs and small waist. A necklace
of flat gold links lay on her cleavage.

"One thing's for sure," Sheffield said, wiping his mouth with
his handkerchief. "The problem isn't the police, it's the press."

Raven squinted through narrowed eyes. The long room had
filled with cigarette smoke.

"How do you figure that? What about the D-notice?"

"That's been lifted, too," said Sheffield. "Molina's arrest means
an entirely new ballgame as far as the Foreign Office is concerned. The last thing they want is to be seen to have prior
knowledge, something that could well turn into an international
incident."

"Come on now," Raven objected. "Cameron's name has never
been mentioned publicly."

Sheffield waved a hand. "That's unimportant. These reporters aren't idiots. They knew there was a story behind the Hans Security robbery—otherwise why all the secrecy? They know that the thieves hired a car. They'll track back and find this address. It's the logical place to start their enquiries."

Kirstie rose, collected the coffee percolator and carried the tray into the kitchen.

"Thanks a lot," Raven said quietly. "That's the last thing she wants to be reminded of, especially after what's already happened. When things move that close, she starts getting nervous."

Sheffield's gesture made light of the criticism. "It'll take some time before they get moving. We'll have Cameron on the plane before then. I know a man at Emirate Airways. The Dubai-Paris-London service turns round at Heathrow. Cameron's on the flight back to Paris."

"It's the police, not the reporters, who worry Kirstie," said Raven. "I know my wife."

"There won't be any problem," said Sheffield. His glass eye gleamed as he leaned forward into the light. "I'm taking Cameron to the airport. There's no need for you people to be involved any longer."

The door buzzer sounded. Cameron's voice sounded in the entryphone. Raven released the door. Kirstie hurried out from the kitchen, glancing sideways as she passed the mirror. They heard Cameron's footsteps coming along the deck. Raven opened the door. The Canadian came into the room, wiping the rain from his face and neck. He peeled off his mac, his grin uncertain as he looked from one to the other.

Raven made the introduction. "Paul Sheffield. He's a friend. He's going to put you on the plane. You're sure that you weren't followed?"

"I wasn't followed," Cameron said shortly. His grin lacked conviction. "Is there any chance of a scotch?"

Kirstie backed off a couple of feet, inspecting the Canadian. "There's blood all over your collar," she said, making a face.

"I cut myself shaving," he said.

Raven poured three fingers of scotch into a tumbler, topped it with water and handed the glass to Cameron. The Canadian sank the contents in one gulp, sat down and shook his head slowly.

"You can't wear that shirt any more," Kirstie complained. "It's filthy." Cameron glanced at his cuffs. "There's a clean one in my bag."

"You don't *have* a bag any longer," Raven said. "I had to get rid of it."

"He can take one of yours," Kirstie said, eyeing her husband.

"Why not?" Raven replied, showing his teeth. "What about pyjamas and a toothbrush?"

He sat down beside his wife, holding his smile.

"Do you know where van Hall is now?"

Cameron emptied his glass and dried his lips on the back of his hand.

"I know where he *was*," he replied. "He was at 132 Kinnerton Street just over an hour ago."

"Have you got the telephone number?" asked Sheffield.

Cameron shook his head. "I think I may have it," said Raven. He gave the number that van Hall had dialed from the Underground station.

Sheffield pulled himself up from the seat. "Can I use the phone in your bedroom?" Raven lifted a hand. Kirstie waited until Sheffield was out of the room.

"He really *is* on our side," she told Cameron.

The Canadian shook his head slowly. "I wish someone would tell me what's going on."

"If those people *were* police at the station, van Hall set you up," Raven said.

Cameron's expression hardened. "I know a cop when I see one. Those guys were plainclothes men."

"It's possible," Raven said. "But you can be sure about one thing. There'd have been a few red faces if you *had* been picked up."

Sheffield was back, sitting in shadow again. "That number doesn't answer. I just had a word with Tomek. He's in the Range Rover at the end of Kinnerton Street. Van Hall won't move a yard without him."

Raven swung round as Cameron opened his mouth. "Don't ask any more bloody questions. Just *listen* for once."

Sheffield looked at the Canadian. "Those things you stole belonged to me," he said. "You don't have to know who I am. All that matters is that other people are involved, government people. Your friend got you into a lot of trouble. Now the thing is to get you off the hook. You're going to sleep here tonight. Tomorrow I'll put you on the plane for Paris. Until then you'll do exactly as you're told. No more disappearances. These people have had enough. They should never have been involved in the first place."

"Understood," Cameron said quietly. He slapped his pockets. "Has anyone got a smoke?"

Raven pushed the package across.

Cameron took out a cigarette and lit it. He extinguished the match and blew smoke through pursed lips.

"I've been doing what I was told since last Sunday night. If it's true that the police don't want me, why don't I just get on the next train for France?"

Raven felt the blood rising, first on his neck then his face. "You seem to have got it into your head that you're some kind of hero. What you are is a thief, my friend, albeit a reluctant one. And a nuisance to everyone here except Kirstie. It would become you to show a little more gratitude."

Kirstie was on her legs quickly. "I'll make up your bed," she told Cameron. "We all need some sleep."

Sheffield said goodnight with old-fashioned courtesy. "Thank you for a delicious meal, Mrs. Raven."

Cameron followed Kirstie along the corridor. Raven took an umbrella from the stand.

"I'll see you out," he said to Sheffield.

The barge floated high on the swollen river. Lights dotted the windows in the other boats. People were preparing for bed. The wind blew the rain at their faces. Raven used the umbrella as a shield. He unfastened the door at the foot of the steps. Lights from above killed his vision.

"Are you sure you'll be all right?" he asked hesitantly.

"I'll be all right," Sheffield replied. "And don't worry about van Hall. There's only one place left for him to go."

Raven pushed the umbrella into Sheffield's hand. "Tomorrow morning, then!"

He locked up and rammed the bolts home. Cameron's door was open. The Canadian was sitting on the side of the bed, a pair of Raven's pyjamas beside him. Water was splashing into the tub in the bathroom.

Kirstie was already under the duvet, no more than her face showing. She stirred in her nest as he put out the light and climbed in beside her. Her whisper was barely audible. "I'm glad you're here."

SIXTEEN

The Chancellor was up on the second floor. Pablo Peralta occupied the two adjoining rooms. The two Chilean girls who worked in the office had gone home three hours earlier. It was eight o'clock in the evening and the rust-coloured velvet curtains were drawn. The windows overlooked a garden where high brick walls enclosed a lawn, flowerbeds and granite chip pathways. Once a year, on the feast day of Saint Iago, the Ambassador and his wife played hosts at an alfresco function for members of the diplomatic corps.

The long room the two men were sitting in ran the width of the building. An array of mirrors increased its size, reflecting the heavy mahogany furniture. The carpet was the same color as the curtains. A pair of shatterglass chandeliers hung from the ceiling like stalactites. There were two French-type pedestal telephones, each with its auxiliary earpiece. Peralta had been in the drawing-room since six o'clock, receiving and making calls from and to Chile. A tray on the table bore the remnants of a meal prepared by the Embassy chef.

Don Enrique Arretega was a short corpulent man in his fifties, wearing a black suit, white collar and shirt and a sober tie. His forehead was broad under layered brown hair. His smile was vague, his prominent eyes attentive. Doña Carmen Arretega's family owned thirty thousand hectares in the north of Chile and was a friend of Pinochet's wife. Arretega had been a career diplomat for eighteen years, surviving Allende's rise and fall without making enemies. Critics claimed that his survival stemmed from the fact that the Ambassador rarely expressed an opinion.

One of the phones rang. Peralta answered it. The switchboard operator spoke from downstairs.

"I have a man on the line, Don Pablo, a foreigner. He wishes to speak to His Excellency. He insists that it is a matter of extreme urgency."

Peralta signaled the Ambassador to pick up the auxiliary earpiece. "His name?" asked Peralta.

The operator did his best to pronounce it. "Rolando van Halla."

"Put him through," said Peralta. The Ambassador tilted his head, creasing his forehead as he concentrated.

The caller's Spanish was grammatically correct but strongly accented. "My name is Roland van Hall, Señor. I must speak to the Ambassador. I apologize for the lateness of the hour but it is a matter of great importance."

Peralta's manner was equally formal. "I am Pablo Peralta, First Secretary. I regret that His Excellency is not available. You may speak to me freely."

A long pause interrupted before van Hall spoke again. "I intend no discourtesy but this is a highly confidential matter."

"If I am to help you," Peralta said patiently, "I must know the nature of your business."

The Ambassador was shifting his weight from one leg to another, frowning.

Van Hall lowered his voice. "I have positive proof of General Molina's complicity in the plot to assassinate President Pinochet."

"Who are you, Señor?" Peralta asked sharply.

"I have already given my name," said van Hall. "I have told you my reason for seeking an interview. That is all you need to know."

Peralta glanced up. The Ambassador's expression offered no clue to his thinking.

"Present yourself here at ten o'clock tomorrow morning," said Peralta. "Ask for me personally. I will do what I can."

"Many thanks," said van Hall. "I can assure you that you will not be disappointed."

Peralta replaced the phone. "Will you inform Santiago or shall I do it, Excellency?"

The Ambassador shrugged. "You are in charge."

General Molina had been arrested that afternoon and transferred to a cell in a sometime Dominican monastery, presently used by the Centro Nacional de Informaciones. His wife and family were under house arrest.

The Ambassador walked over to the fireplace. He stood for a moment, staring down at the glow from the artificial logs. He swung round suddenly.

"Betrayal by a friend is a grievous burden for the President to bear."

Peralta reached for the cigarette box. He said nothing.

The Ambassador rocked on his heels. "Have the people arrived from Santiago?"

"An hour ago," said Peralta. "They are in the Cumberland Hotel. I supposed that you would not wish to see them."

The Ambassador's uplifted hand fended off the possibility. "No, no!" he said hurriedly. "I trust there will be no violence. You know my feelings on the subject. It would make my position untenable."

"Have no fear, Don Enrique," Peralta said reassuringly.

The Ambassador's expression was doubtful. "Do you still think you can persuade this man to testify against Molina?"

Peralta nodded. Arretega was adept at avoiding responsibility. "Everything Raven told us about van Hall has proved accurate. The man is a cunning and venal adventurer. Someone who is clever enough to try to make capital out of failure. His call here proves it. I think he will agree to give evidence. In fact I am sure of it."

"Perhaps I should know more about this proposition of yours," said the Ambassador.

Peralta's shoulders rose and fell. "It is simple enough. Molina's trial will be open for all to attend. The riffraff of the world will be present. Newspaper reporters, international meddlers, people from the Council of Churches. Observers from every left wing organisation you can think of. Justice must be seen to be done with van Hall the star witness."

"And if he refuses?"

Peralta's smile was bleak. "He is going to ask for a great deal of money. The equation is simple. No testimony, no money."

The Ambassador's frown dragged his whole face with it. "If this man agrees, the eyes of the world will be on him. He will be a guest in our country. Nothing must happen to him."

"If van Hall comes to Chile, nothing *will* happen to him," said Peralta. "We must view this matter in proper perspective, Excellency. The money Molina has stolen no longer matters in spite of whatever the Banco de Chile might say. What is of much deeper concern is the extent of Molina's treachery, his readiness to use people with Communist connections. If van Hall gives testimony, Molina's link with the left is established."

"And van Hall?" queried the Ambassador. "What happens to him at the end of all this?"

Peralta showed his good teeth. "We leave him to God's tender mercy."

Arretega changed the subject. "Have you spoken with Raven again?"

"No," said Peralta. "He is the only one who could cause trouble. I have taken the liberty of suggesting that the contribution he spoke of would be a wise investment. I am waiting for authorization for Your Excellency to disburse the funds."

The Ambassador stomped a few steps, speaking as he went. "In the event of God's tender mercy failing, Pablo, nothing rash must be done. Do I make myself clear?"

Peralta smiled. "As always."

The Ambassador grunted. "This whole business worries me, Pablo. I wish it belonged to somebody else."

"It does," said Peralta. "It belongs to me. Have no fear, Don Enrique."

The Ambassador placed his hand on the younger man's shoulder. "Just be careful, for my sake as well as your own."

SEVENTEEN

Van Hall rolled over in bed and reached for the button on the bedside lamp. It was ten minutes past seven by his watch. Years of practice made getting up easy for him. Early morning calls had come in many strange places. He flexed his muscles tentatively and drew back the curtains. Street lamps shone on empty pavements. The rain had stopped although damp still filmed the tops of parked cars. He went into the bathroom. The mirror showed the division between what was left of his suntan and his normal skin color. He shaved, wrapped himself in a bath sheet and collected the newspapers from the hallway. He spread them out on the kitchen table and leafed through the pages as the coffee bubbled on the stove. There was nothing of interest to him except an agency report.

PINOCHET AIDE ARRESTED IN SANTIAGO

It was a bald account dealing with Molina's arrest. There were no details given. He toasted a slice of brown bread and had breakfast listening to the eight o'clock news on the radio. At a quarter to nine he went upstairs and took care with his choice of attire. He selected a dark blue suit, white shirt and grey tie. South Americans set great store on appearance. A normal ebullience had replaced his overnight gloom. He had what these people needed. It no longer mattered who he dealt with.

It was ten minutes past nine when he rang Brompton Central Cleaners.

"This is Mister van Hall from Kinnerton Street. I'd like you to send someone round to the house this morning."

There was a rustle of papers as the girl consulted her files. "Yes, I have the address, Mister van Hall. You realize that it isn't your normal day for service?"

"I know that," he answered. "I'll be out of the country for a while. I'd like a clean house to come back to. Can you manage to do that for me?"

She consulted her records again. "I think we can manage that. Would sometime this morning suit you?"

"Any time," he said. "I might be out but you've got a set of keys. Tell the men to leave your account in the kitchen table along with the keys."

He had no idea when he would be back in England. The Jaguar was already stored in a long-term parking garage.

A cab dropped him outside the Chilean Embassy just before ten o'clock. He climbed the steps to the heavy front door. A man and a woman were standing on the basement steps below, waiting for the consulate-general to open. Van Hall rang the doorbell. A squat dark-complexioned man answered the summons. Van Hall spoke in Spanish.

"I am Señor van Hall. I have an appointment with Señor Peralta."

The servant opened the door. Daylight streamed into the hallway. Van Hall followed the servant up a stairway decorated with oil paintings commemorating the Conquistadores. The servant knocked on a cream-painted door and turned the handle. He stood to one side, closing the door as van Hall entered the room.

A man rose from his chair and came forward with outstretched hand. He was in his mid-thirties, elegantly dressed, with a thin narrow head and a highbridged nose. His smile barely altered the shape of his mouth.

"Señor van Hall! I am Pablo Peralta." He waved to a chair. "Please take a seat."

Van Hall removed his overcoat and placed it on the couch beside him. He leaned back and took the weight of his legs on his heels.

"I regret that His Excellency has been called to a meeting," Peralta said. "But you may speak to me in complete confidence."

Van Hall was a veteran of hours spent in ministerial annexes. He was accustomed to the indifference shown to members of the public. The room they were in looked like part of a museum. There was the same stiff formality, the impression that paintings and furniture were there only to be viewed. There was a glimpse of a garden beyond the windows.

Peralta got to his feet.

"If I understand you correctly, you have information that you think might be of interest to us. Is this correct?"

Van Hall wriggled deeper into the cushions. "I am a business-man, Señor Peralta. What I have is for sale. If not to you then to somebody else. I give you first offer."

Peralta glanced at his watch. "Would you like me to order cof-fee?"

Van Hall shook his head. "I do not have much time. Let there be no doubt about it, Señor Peralta. My sole interest in this mat-ter is money. I have positive proof of General Molina's involve-ment in the attempt on Pinochet's life."

The room was suddenly quiet, the only sound a faint clatter of office machinery from somewhere nearby. Peralta resumed his seat.

"I admire your directness," he said. "I will try to be equally frank. What is this proof that you offer?"

"Molina has a godson living in Paris, a man called Ortega who handles the general's finances. I have a photocopy of a check drawn on Ortega's business account for the equivalent of half-a-million pounds sterling. The check is payable to a so-called secu-rity firm."

Peralta considered his fingernails. "Then perhaps you should offer your wares to Ortega." A telephone rang. Peralta ignored it.

"Ortega is no longer in Paris," van Hall said.

"So you give us first refusal?" Peralta was smiling again.

"First chance to buy," van Hall amended. "Ortega clearly has problems. It will take time to locate him."

Peralta opened a lapis-lazuli box and extracted a cigarette. He rolled it, changing its shape from oval to round. He bent over his lighter. "This check," he said, exhaling. "Do you have it with you?"

Van Hall chuckled. "You are not being serious."

Peralta waved his cigarette. "You may have come here with a cock-and-bull story. We would require convincing evidence."

Van Hall maintained his composure. "Let us be frank. My presence here establishes my bona fides. The evidence you need can be produced within the hour. All I want is your agreement to pay my price."

"And what is your price?" the First Secretary asked through a barrage of smoke.

"Three million pounds sterling," said van Hall.

"That is a great deal of money," Peralta said, pinching the words together. "Would you be prepared to make a statement?"

Van Hall's forehead creased. "You mean here, at the Embassy?"

"In a Chilean court," said Peralta. "Failing that, it seems to me that whatever you offer is worthless."

Van Hall's laugh was strained. "You are asking me to appear in a Chilean court?"

"Why not?" said Peralta. "Measures will be taken to protect all government witnesses."

Van Hall ran the film in his head. Fans whirled. Television cameras panned. The courtroom was full of armed men and reporters.

"I'd need to consider my answer," he said.

Peralta extinguished his cigarette. "We would be willing to guarantee your safe conduct to Chile and back again."

"I need time to consider," van Hall said obstinately.

"I understand," said Peralta. "Perhaps you will give me your telephone number. I am sure that His Excellency will wish to speak to you personally."

Van Hall detached a card from his wallet and placed it on top of the bright blue cigarette box. He picked up his overcoat. "I shall be in the house for the rest of the day. Adiós, Señor Peralta."

The uniformed servant opened the door to the street. Van Hall walked until a cab stopped for his signal.

"Kinnerton Street," he said, and closed his eyes, smiling.

The interview had taken no more than forty minutes. The men from the cleaners had not yet been. Van Hall filled the kettle. He took the mug of coffee through to his study and switched on the answering machine. Only one message was recorded. His secretary's voice sounded bored. "Mister Sarakakis from Chemical Bank phoned twice today. He wants you to call him soonest on Extension Twenty-Six."

Van Hall pressed the button, erasing the message. The sharks smelled blood. The bank held the deeds to the house and good luck to them. Property values in the southeast had already peaked. A forced sale would fall well short of his mortgage, remortgage and unpaid interest. He had no regrets at the prospect of losing Kinnerton Street. England had been his base for too long. It was time to move on. He had no clear idea where to head for. It didn't matter. Given money and a convincing passport, he could survive anywhere.

He finished his coffee, thinking back to Peralta. You bet they would like him to appear in a Chilean court! His testimony would carry weight with the independent observers who would flock to the show-trial. It wouldn't matter if Molina disclaimed all knowledge of him. No-one expected the truth from the General.

Van Hall unlocked the drawer in his desk and pulled out the envelope Raven had delivered. The contents had already been through too many hands. Just a few pieces of paper, worthless if found on the street. In spite of what he had said to Peralta, his feelings about going to Chile were ambivalent.

He turned in the chair as the doorbell rang. It was typical that the cleaners would have forgotten to bring the keys with them. He put the envelope back in the drawer and went out to the hallway. He released the catch on the Ingersoll lock. Two men moved in quickly from the street, pushing van Hall in front of them. One of them closed the door. Both men wore wraparound sunglasses and stone-coloured raincoats over peg-top trousers. Each carried a Spanish-made thirty-eight-millimeter automatic pistol. The taller of the two used the barrel of his gun as a prod, pushing van Hall back into the study. The shorter man drew the curtains, shutting out the light from the street. His companion picked up the whisky decanter from the drinks shelf. Each movement seemed to have been rehearsed. The man with the decanter found a cut-glass tumbler and filled it with whisky. His partner moved behind van Hall's chair. Van Hall felt the gun digging into his neck. The man holding the whisky glass unscrewed a phial and emptied some tablets into the tumbler. He swirled the glass and used a pen to stir the mixture. Sweat broke out on van Hall's body, cold, as it dripped on his ribcage.

Metal fillings in the man's mouth gleamed as he spoke. *"Toma!"* he ordered.

Van Hall attempted to rise from the chair. Strong hands forced him down again.

"There is no need," van Hall said desperately.

The pills were reduced to a sediment at the bottom of the glass. The man facing van Hall stirred the mixture again, this time using a gloved forefinger. He leaned across the desk, forcing the rim of the glass between van Hall's lips.

"Toma!" he repeated.

The glass tilted. A hand from behind seized van Hall's hair and dragged his head back. Another hand held his jaws open. His mouth gaped until the last of the drink was poured down his gullet. The two men watched as he keeled from the chair. The empty glass rolled across the desk. His ears popped and his vision blurred. He opened his mouth but no sound came from it. He pitched sideways suddenly, striking his head on the edge of the desk as he fell to the floor.

He was dead when the shorter man stepped over him and opened the curtains again. The intruders let themselves out to the street.

EIGHTEEN

The *Albatross* had lowered on the ebbing tide until the flat-bottomed hull rested on mud. The new position brought an unaccustomed stability to those on board. Raven and Cameron were sitting at the kitchen table, the remnants of the meal that Kirstie had cooked for them on the table. That done, she retreated back into the bedroom, pleading a loss of appetite. Raven sensed the real reason. They had been tiptoeing around one another since early morning, avoiding the subject of Cameron's impending departure. Of the three, Cameron seemed most at ease. A night's rest had restored his self-confidence. He removed the toothpick from his mouth and placed it in the ashtray.

"What was the name of that airline again?"

"Emirate Airways," said Raven. He took the dirty plates to the sink-board and resumed his seat at the table. Music was playing in the bedroom.

Cameron took a look at the clock on the kitchen dresser. He was wearing a blue-striped shirt that belonged to Raven.

"How long does it take to get to the airport?"

Raven let his breath go. "Have you always been like this?" he asked suddenly.

Cameron locked both hands behind his head, smiling. "I'm not too sure what that means."

It was too late for Raven to pull back. "Thinking of yourself all the time. *Using* people."

Cameron's glance was level. "I always give good value."

"Get out of here," Raven said. "You disgust me."

Cameron pushed his chair back. The bedroom door closed behind him.

It was another half-hour before the entrance buzzer sounded. Kirstie and Cameron came into the sitting room. Raven opened the door to the deck. The morning air was sharp with the muddy smell of the foreshore. Gulls patrolled overhead, raucous and quarrelsome. Sheffield appeared. He stood in the doorway, looking across the room at Cameron.

"Are you ready?" he asked.

Cameron glanced round, smiling. With the exception of Raven's shirt, the Canadian was dressed as he had been four days before. The green corduroy suit needed pressing again.

Kirstie had put her hair up in coils. She was wearing black velvet trousers, a white shirt and ballet shoes.

She smiled at Sheffield. "You look tired." Her voice was sympathetic.

Sheffield shrugged. "I didn't get much sleep."

"Peralta called," Raven said. "They're making the contribution. He didn't say how much. All he asked was how the payment should be made."

"Van Hall's dead," Sheffield said.

The grin vanished on Cameron's face. Kirstie covered her eyes with her hands.

"It isn't a pretty story." Sheffield pushed his cigarette into the ashtray.

Kirstie hurried out of the room. Raven shrugged as the kitchen door closed. "She doesn't like violence."

Sheffield nodded understandingly. "Tomek saw the whole thing. He was in the Range Rover. He could see the Chilean Embassy from where he was parked. He saw van Hall arrive and then leave. Tomek followed him back to Kinnerton Street."

Raven glanced along the corridor. The kitchen door had been partially opened.

"What happened?" he asked.

"Van Hall was there in the house alone. A couple of guys arrived shortly afterwards. Van Hall opened the door for them. They were in the house for ten, fifteen minutes, then they came out again. They separated as soon as they were outside. One went off in the direction of Wilton Place, the other one walked right past the Range Rover. There's this arcade at the bottom of Kinnerton Street. Tomek watched the whole thing from there. A van arrived at the house from a firm of contract cleaners. They had keys to the house. They went in and came out again within seconds. That's when all hell broke loose. An ambulance arrived with a couple of police cars. Tomek counted twelve people in the house at one time. They brought van Hall out on a stretcher, a blanket over his head. There were people standing around on the street by this time. Tomek had a word with one of the cleaners. He said they'd found van Hall lying on the floor, an empty pill box by his side."

The room was suddenly quiet. Cameron broke the silence. "You mean he was murdered."

Sheffield lifted his head. He looked at his watch. "It's time we made a move."

Kirstie was back in the sitting room. Cameron stood in front of her, staring down at her face. He bent and kissed her on both cheeks.

"Goodbye, pussycat," he said softly.

"Goodbye," she answered. "You'll understand if John and I don't come to the airport."

"I'll be sorry," he said, looking down at her again. "But I'll understand." He transferred his gaze to Raven.

For a moment it seemed that he was about to offer his hand but thought better of it. "Goodbye," he repeated awkwardly. "I'll call you both from Paris."

Raven said nothing.

The Canadian shrugged and stepped out on deck. Sheffield gathered his hat and coat.

"Don't worry about a thing. I'll see him on the plane. Everything's under control. I'll talk to you later."

Raven rammed both bolts home. It was twenty minutes to ten.

"Well, that's that, I hope," he said.

She drew a long breath. "If you're not going to need your word processor, I could use it in the studio."

"Anything that makes you happy," he said.

He followed her into the guest room and tore the piece of paper from the wall.

BEGINNING   MIDDLE   END

He crumpled it into a ball and dropped it in the waste-basket. He sat on the end of the bed. A pair of dirty socks on the floor was the only relic of Cameron's presence. When he looked up, Kirstie was watching him from the doorway.

"Do you find me sexy?" he asked, his expression serious.

She subjected him to a long hard stare. "I've never really thought about it," she said. Her face was equally sober. "I suppose you have your moments."

He pushed himself up and came close to her. Her eyes were as clear as a north Ontario trout-stream. A pulse beat erratically under the skin on her throat.

"You know that I love you," he said very softly.

She nodded. "I know," she replied.

He wrapped an arm around her shoulders and led her towards their bedroom. It was as though the last ten days had never happened.